THE PATH OF TIME

Kenny Emmanuel

THE PATH OF TIME

This is a work of fiction. All of the characters, organizations, and events portrayed in this novel are either products of the author's imagination or are used fictitiously.

Copyright © 2022 by Kenny Emmanuel

Cover Art by Eddy Shinjuku
Cover Layout and Graphic Design by Felipe Conde

ISBN 979-8-9863367-1-8

Special thanks to Jared Austin, Michelle F., Shirley B. Garrett, Bailey Gouzie, Brent Graves, Lisa Prince, Ed Stockton, Debbie Yutko, and the North Alabama Science Fiction and Cake Appreciation Society (NASFCAS)

Dedicated to the love of my life... Wherever you are... Whenever you are...

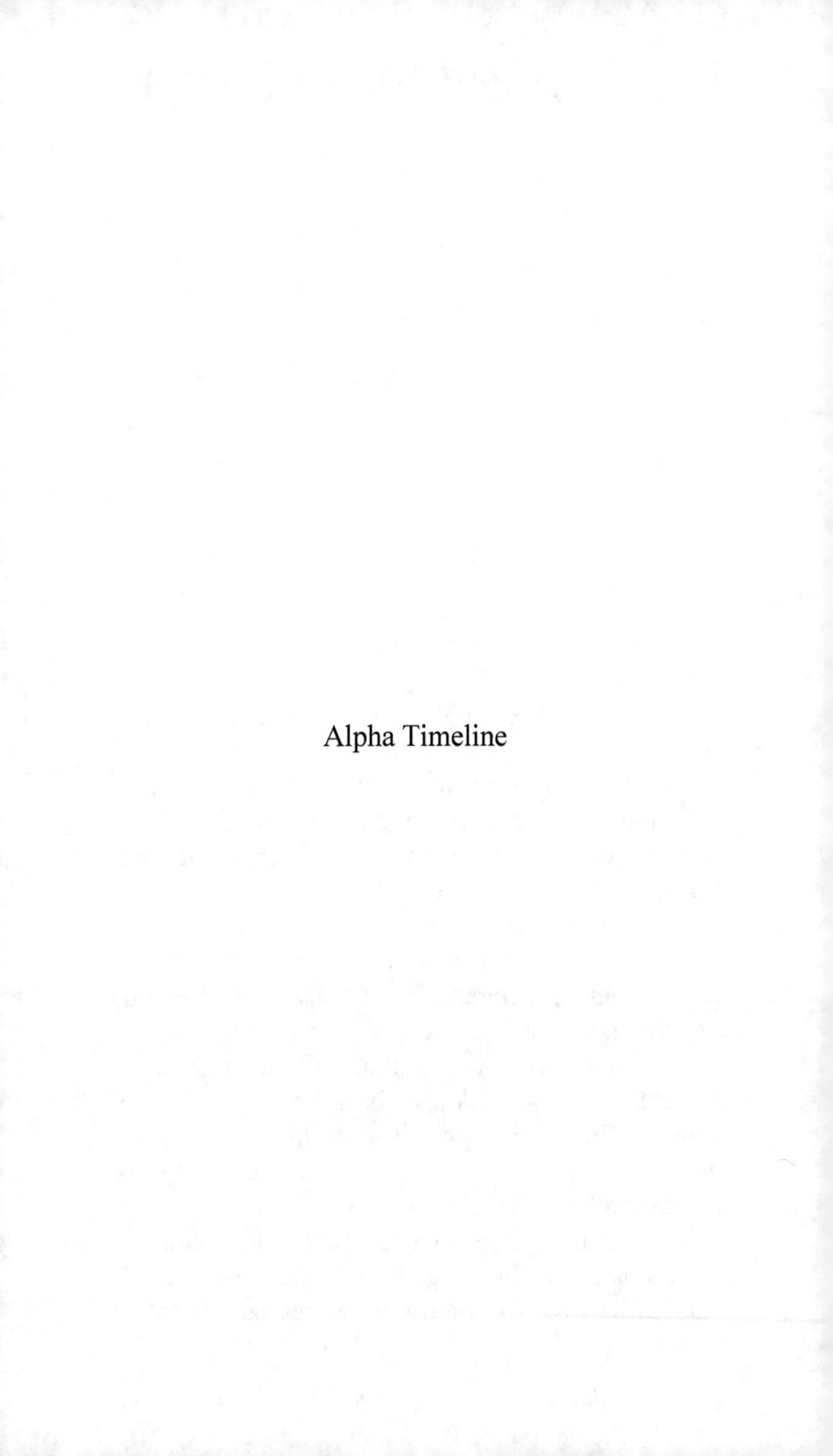

Alpha Timeline

A.1 Path of Love

The love of my life doesn't exist in this space-time…

That's the subtitle of the stream I started with the equipment I'd set up in my garage. Fewer than five viewers watched me start down the path of love. Some people already meandered, paraded, and even skipped down their versions of the path I sought, as defined by their logic, emotions, and upbringing. My path would be different, but if we were to agree on one thing, it's that the path can be a perilous one.

A single correct path among trillions seemed unfathomable. I would know, because I struggled for years to find it. But what if it lay in the past, and I had missed it? What if it existed in a future, yet to be discovered?

My solution required a new, uncharted path.

I took a deep breath and stared at my computer's camera lens as if I could see the people who often watched me recite poems, sing songs, and engage in amateur rap. Instead of their faces, their pleasant comments helped me find my voice.

In my best announcer impersonation, I said, "Yo, it's your boy, Kieran." I laughed at the silly faced emojis posted in the comments. The viewers agreed: that wasn't me. I scratched the scruff of my chin and started over in a normal tone. "Good evening, ladies and gentlemen. Tonight, I'll take the next step toward the path of love. I'll say it again: The love of my life doesn't exist in this space-time. So, I'm going to find her in another."

I pushed back from the white plastic folding table. The wheels of my office chair clattered against the concrete garage floor. I swung aside to show my viewers a platform flanked by two eight-foot-tall objects covered by white sheets. Cables of varying thicknesses and colors snaked from beneath the fabric and disappeared into the darkness at the edges of the room.

With a satisfied breath, I pushed myself out of the comfortable mesh chair and strode to the first sheet. In a grandiose pose, and with every intention to reveal the artifact underneath in a dramatic manner, I paused. I was about to open Pandora's box. What I hesitated to unveil could transform the world overnight—no, immediately, depending on how fast the world realized what a self-proclaimed romantic had accomplished.

I didn't even know if the damn thing worked, but logging every success was just as important as recording every failure.

I tossed both sheets aside and revealed four pillars, two on each side of the platform, to my world of six. Their tops extended above the camera's field of view and stopped a foot beneath the ceiling. I admired the closest pair before returning to the chair. I spun to face the computer and stroked several keys in rapid succession. The pillars came alive. Energy spiraled upward, sparking as the demand for current increased. Their reflections on the monitor, the flickering lights I should've warned my viewers about, and the crackling sounds worried me until the surging energy calmed.

The tension in my shoulders relaxed. "Don't worry, folks. Electronic systems can draw a lot of current when first turned on." The system boot was the least of my concerns. I still hadn't engaged the primary function, which, by my calculations, could cause a neighborhood blackout if my safety measures failed.

"I'm ready," I said. "Project Title: Path of Love. Time: 0055 hours. The initial run will begin at 0100 hours. The first objective is to open and connect two points in space across a distance of ten feet. The second objective is to send an object from one point to the other, unscathed. The third objective is to extend the range of the gateway beyond Earth. I expect the final objective to fail, primarily due to power limitations. I also expect the gateway to maintain an opening for less than a second. However, if I can get a glimpse of some other place—some other world—it will be a success. I have a high-speed camera with a trigger pulse in line with system activation. I can't stream high-speed videos to social media, so you'll have to check it out later."

The comments supported me. Three of the five viewers wished me luck. One viewer, with the username SerialData, seemed excited with fingers crossed and a thumbs-up emoji, followed by a casual warning: "Don't end up in a black hole, bro."

I smiled and raised two thumbs at the camera. "Don't worry, I accounted for my position, Earth's rotation, and the spatial coordinates of every known planet, asteroid field, and black hole."

No additional comments followed.

"T-minus one minute," I said. At thirty seconds remaining, "Initializing Path of Love. Authentication: Whiskey Tango Foxtrot."

The system hummed louder, but without the chaotic energy of boot up.

"Three… Two… One… Engage!"

The garage lights flickered once. The system screamed for a moment before it settled down to a steady hum. I stood, mesmerized by the prismatic light along the sides of the pillars.

I grabbed my test subject: a worn-down tennis ball I'd bounced off the garage walls during sessions of deep thought. At the center of the platform, I peered between the two pillars on the right and saw the back of my head—an infinite number of them. Excitement filled me.

I hurled my test subject between the two pillars. It smacked me in the back of the head. Ah, sweet revenge. Another good sign that the system worked.

My patience for proper procedures and annotations vanished. I doubled back to the computer, scrolled past a list of complex numbers, and verified that the chosen coordinates were not among them. I hurriedly entered the new destination's coordinates, and without a countdown, I hit enter. The garage lights flickered once more….

Bravo Timeline

B.1 Path of Michael

"I'm ready," I said. "Project Title: Path of Love. Time: 0055 hours. The initial run will begin at 0100 hours. The first objective is to open and connect two points in space across a distance of ten feet. The second objective is to send an object from one point to the other, unscathed. The third objective is to extend the range of the gateway beyond Earth. I expect the final objective to fail, primarily due to power limitations. I also expect the gateway to maintain an opening for less than a second. However, if I can get a glimpse of some other place—some other world—it will be a success. I have a high-speed camera with a trigger pulse in line with system activation. I can't stream high-speed videos to social media, so you'll have to check it out later."

The comments supported me. Four of the five viewers wished me luck. One viewer, with the username SerialData, seemed excited with fingers crossed and a thumbs-up emoji, followed by a question: "Who's that behind you?"

I whipped my head around. A man sat at the center of the platform with legs partially crossed, his right knee raised to the height of his chest, and his right arm hanging over it at the elbow.

"Yo," he greeted me with a smile and a wave of the hand. "Before you destroy the world again, I have a proposition for you."

I stood and stumbled backward against the desk, its contents similarly disturbed. *Who is he? How did he get in?* The front door's alarm hadn't sounded. I considered using my phone to check the camera installed there, but didn't want to provoke him. I'd purposely stationed my desk in front of the stairs leading up to the rest of the house, so he couldn't have come down them and walked past me unseen. He couldn't have entered through the garage door. I would've seen and heard it rattling open. *Where did he come from?*

"You mind turning that thing off? I'm camera shy." He nodded at the stream.

I shook my head, more by instinct than logic. Logic would have argued that he was far too beautiful to be camera shy. He had sky-blue eyes emboldened by slick, black strands of hair that faded into a perfectly edged beard. His dark blue outfit resembled a flight suit out of a science-fiction television show.

He raised a brow. "Surely, you don't think the world will be your witness. If history has taught us anything, it's that humans only act in their own self-interest. They'll only defend you if they have something to gain." He glanced at the pillars to his right. "I suppose they would have something to gain."

The man was at home with a confident smile behind his demigod appearance. There wasn't a hint of concern in his posture or demeanor while I stood frozen in place. But the longer he sat in front of me, the more my eyes adjusted to his presence. I noticed little things like the abundance of pockets and empty straps adorning his long-sleeved attire. A partially obscured insignia stitched above his left breast. And the lack of a weapon.

What am I afraid of?

I calmed down and found the courage to respond. "I'm more worried about what *you* have to gain than the five people watching this stream."

"Five?" The man touched an index finger to his right temple. "Ah yeah, I suppose we're still at T-minus. At T-plus, you'll have several hundred thousand viewers, which means the FBI will show up in…seven minutes and forty seconds."

My body shifted toward the stairs, another uncommanded move. *Calm down! Stop getting caught up in his pace. In the game of love, this is the guy we always lose to—the nonchalant, charismatic—*

"You didn't think you could open a hole in space without turning some heads, did ya? The government already controls the dirt you walk on, the water you drink, and the air you breathe. Did you think they wouldn't seek to control the space you occupy?"

He stood. Six feet tall, confirmed when he walked to the pillar on his right and caressed the top of it with his arm fully extended. Then, before I realized, he was halfway to me.

"We've wasted a lot of time," he said, "so I'll get to the point. In approximately six minutes, the FBI will blast your garage door open. They'll blind you with bright lights, drown your pleas with vocal commands, and so on. You'll destroy the machine before they abduct you. They'll demand you build another, but you're a good guy, so you'll refuse to cooperate because tech like this in military hands is world-ending. Then they'll torture you to your final breath. You'll die. Alone. Stripped of humanity. In a hole unknown even to me." He stopped in front of me and leaned past me to shut down the stream. "But we can change that."

I didn't stop him. I couldn't. His new position revealed a gun holstered on his right hip. The remaining straps were indeed empty. The insignia I had thought obscured by his seated position looked haphazardly torn off, as if he stole the outfit and didn't want to be associated with whatever the uniform represented, but couldn't be bothered to disassociate himself completely.

"Um, you said something about destroying the world again. What did you mean?"

He straightened. "You opened a doorway to a black hole. The rest is science."

"Oh…God," I whispered as I crumpled, horrified at the thought of having ended the world. My right elbow on top of the desk prevented me from collapsing to the floor.

"On the bright side," he said, "everyone died in an instant. They probably never felt a thing. There are worse ways to go. And so we're on the same page, I don't plan on dying with you. I also don't plan on getting caught by the goon squad."

If I destroyed the world, where did he come from?

"Are you…from the future?" I blurted out. "If the world ended, how are you here?"

He clapped several times. "Bingo! You created a new timeline, which is fucking incredible.

Throughout history, only groups of people, movements, atrocities, and etcetera, have created new timelines. But you created one all by yourself. So yeah, I'm from the timeline that wasn't dragged into oblivion." He turned his head and blew at the few strands of hair that obstructed his view of me. "Four minutes."

Panic surfaced in my voice. "What more do you want from me? You prevented me from ending the world, right? The future's changed."

He laughed as he walked toward the platform. He spoke away from me. "I'm not here to save your world, reset the timeline, change the past, or any of that crap, and there's no evidence those actions would impact the future—my future, anyway. Maybe I'll be special like you and create a new timeline, but that's not why I'm here." His voice trailed off as he spoke more to himself than to me.

"Why *are* you here?"

He turned to face me. "I need your help to change my present, which is far more doable than any of the other time travel shenanigans. It's simple. I'll help you find the love of your life if you help me save the love of mine. Because yours doesn't exist in this space-time, right? Here's your chance to find her in another." He extended his right hand toward me. His confident smile invited me, too.

Noting my hesitation, he added, "It's me or the goon squad."

His sudden appearance was the only reason I had to believe him. Then the front door's alarm buzzed. My phone did, too. I pulled the device out of my pocket, and in typical fashion, the security app required me to enter a complex password instead of using the quicker facial recognition feature.

He snapped his fingers. "Right on time. Your choice, kid. I really will leave you behind. My damsel in distress is waiting for me. One minute."

I slipped the phone into my pocket and ran up to the platform. I didn't take his hand, but I stood next to him and mumbled, "This is crazy. Wait, I didn't set the system to overload."

He grabbed my shoulder and pulled me back. "I'll take care of it. You sit back, keep your hands and feet inside the vehicle, and enjoy the ride."

He raised his left arm and pulled the sleeve back to reveal a five-inch-wide vambrace illuminated with digital overlays that displayed equations, graphs, and sequences I had never seen before. He rotated the edges of the arm guard, tapped the screen several times, and hit the large "ENGAGE" button on the display. A countdown started at five.

"Since you're a goody two shoes, I'll call you Michael. And since you consider me the lesser of two evils, you can call me Lucifer. We'll be team archangels."

Puzzled, I asked, "If Lucifer is the lesser of two evils, who is the greater?"

"God."

B.2 Path of Lucifer

I didn't feel a thing, especially afterward. Light receded to normal levels as I fell to my knees and then face first toward the concrete. An arm prevented me from meeting the god Lucifer had spoken of before the light had enveloped us.

As my senses stabilized, I asked, "What did you do to me?" It took all the strength I had to part my lips for the words.

"Nothing." The vocal vibrations above traveled away from me. "Your sense of time is distorted. Think of it as extreme jet lag."

He lifted my right arm over his shoulder and dragged me toward a mattress atop a black metal frame shoved against a familiar gray wall.

"Where are we?"

"Your garage." Lucifer settled me on the bed. "Welcome home."

The lighting was much better than in my garage. There weren't any dark corners, but I still felt shadows watching me. I stared at a gray ceiling devoid of any unique qualities and wished he would've placed my head in a more interesting direction.

I attempted to move my body, but it refused. Some areas twitched, giving me faith that I wasn't paralyzed. I moved my eyes to their corners and saw a couple of columns similar to my spatial gateway. Multiple loose cables dangled over the few connected ones. For a moment, I thought I was still at home and that Lucifer had drugged and kidnapped me before sabotaging the gateway to make me believe I was somewhere else. Or he had just sabotaged my gateway. If he couldn't have it, then nobody else could, either. But then I noticed that the garage door was missing. A normal door stood off-center to the left. I strained my eyes too much, and a frustrated breath escaped me.

"You better not be dying on me," Lucifer said.

The sound of liquid flowing into a cup followed. A strong aroma filled the air, its rich flavor pushing the scent of desolation aside. I was certain the smell was coffee. Then I heard a scraping noise of something dragged across the concrete. Lucifer entered the edge of my vision with a chair and sat. He pulled up his left sleeve and revealed the vambrace, the one that had supposedly produced enough energy to send us forward in time. How, exactly, I didn't know.

"I bet you're wondering how this thing works." Lucifer rotated his forearm back and forth. "Honestly, I don't know. The engineering is beyond me, and I'm terrible at math. I didn't make it, but I need you to make something similar. Instead of manipulating time, I need to manipulate space."

"I thought…save…love…" I weakly muttered.

Lucifer took a slurp of his drink. "Yes, that is the goal." He paused for a moment. "The love of my life, Evelyn, has been taken by TIME, the Temporal Interdimensional Multidimensional Entity. Say that ten times fast. Actually, I can do that. I can speed up the time required to tell you my story. Then I can adjust the time the words take to reach you." Lucifer seemed proud of his revelation. "Here, let me show you," he said and moved out of my field of vision.

I was confused, but couldn't object. My muscles refused to execute my commands, although they continued to show signs of improvement.

"Please, don't get up," Lucifer said. He was out of sight, but his voice was next to me as if he'd never left. "And please, don't interrupt. You'll miss some important information."

I relaxed. Not that many other options were viable. Strange as the situation was, I understood what was happening. I closed my eyes and focused on his words.

Lucifer's disembodied voice said, "Eve was taken by TIME, an entity that polices aspects of timelines both temporal and spatial. Supposedly, changing the past doesn't change the future of that timeline. However, it can create a new, unnatural timeline—an Artificial Timeline. TIME doesn't believe man should have such power. I think it means more work for the entity who would prefer to sit on its collective ass.

"How often do people fuck with the timelines, anyway? Through my research, investigations, and the occasional interrogation, I learned that the life of a timeline is like that of a person. Tens of thousands are born every day. Tens of thousands die every day.

Some deaths are natural due to cosmic events, and others are unexpected due to the ignorance of some idiot like you…," the voice lowered to a whisper as it finished the sentence, "and like Eve.

"I loved her more than any other existence in the universe, yet she found a way to love me more. We both wanted our time to last forever, but only she could make that reality. The best I could do was find us a nice little house with a breathtaking view. She created a temporal bubble around the property where the flow of time inside differed from the outside. When supplies ran low, we stepped out, got what we needed, and returned. I watched the people in the nearest town grow old. I bought apples from their kids, bagged by their grandkids. Life was perfect."

Lucifer's voice continued, anger building in the delayed signal. "Until TIME showed up in gray robes that masked their face, shape, and intent. After all the human atrocities they stood by and watched, they chose to end our happily ever after. TIME is not in the business of tampering with the natural, temporal flow of existence—or some bullshit like that.

"That's what they said when they took her from me. I fought back, but I didn't stand a chance. I tried to use the bracelet, but it was only a prototype. Eve had planned to slow down time outside the house, too. She strived to eternalize every second we spent together. I used it to fight back, but it wasn't enough to wield time as a power." The voice stopped.

In the silence that followed, I let the words of his story sink in, imagining every moment. With some effort, I turned my head toward the center of the room. Lucifer hunched over a metal desk connected to several others, all of them overlooked by arrays of monitors with too much information for me to process.

He must have noticed me looking at him and said, "They destroyed our paradise, but worse, they trampled on our love." He grabbed his left forearm. "They held me high off the ground by this arm, threatening to take either it or the device. They said in a singular voice, 'Leave it, his love is not enough to overcome reality.' Those words echoed in my ears for nearly a century, the bubble of time *they* imprisoned me within." Lucifer turned his head toward me. "Help me, Michael. I need power over the spatial domain to fight TIME and save Eve."

I turned away. What he asked for was impossible. That was what I wanted to think, but it wasn't too long ago that I thought spatial travel was a dream, and that time travel was science fiction. Lucifer wasn't asking me to fight TIME. He was asking me to give him the means to fight them. But I worried about the dangers of getting involved. I wondered if TIME would target me if I helped. I wondered if they even existed.

I swallowed hard. "You're asking me to…look, it's one thousand percent a tragedy what happened to you and Eve. I want to help, but…," I was at a loss for words. There was no excuse short of cowardice.

"But you're afraid." Lucifer smiled in defeat. "I get it. I really do, but you'll have to face them, eventually. We stand a better chance together."

Shock jolted through me. I almost raised a knee. "What do you mean?"

"Kid, you ended a timeline. The torture I spoke of earlier. Stripped of humanity. In a hole unknown even to me. That would be TIME punishing you in some unreachable dimension for erasing a quintillion or so lives."

"Eight billion," I said to lessen the severity of my actions. My stomach clenched.

"Well, excuse me, mister honor fucking roll."

I continued, raising my voice little by little to drown the potential truth he spoke. "And that wasn't me! You stopped me. That other me died along with…" I fought against reality. "Did it even really happen?"

Lucifer laughed. "Oh, it happened, all right. Whether it was you or your dimensional counterpart, they'll punish and erase your existence across all timelines. When you spot an ant, do you kill the one, or do you kill every single ant you can find? The entire colony, right? Because if you leave one alive, they'll come marching down the same path."

I had pushed myself too hard. Breathing hurt. I tried to keep the pain from my voice. "What about you? You're alive and—"

"Kid, you don't want to be where I was. Death would have been far better than a century of loneliness, guilt, hate, anger, rage, regret. I'd throw a dictionary at you if I had one, but there aren't enough words in that thing to explain the time I existed, if one can even call it existing."

I closed my eyes, reopening them when I felt Lucifer's presence. He sat on the edge of the bed with his back to me. "It's whatever though. I'll return you to your time."

A moment of silence passed. Lucifer didn't get up, and I hadn't officially tendered my resignation. I opened my mouth but held back the words until I knew he was listening. He tilted his head. Almost unnoticeably, had I not been studying him. "If they erased me across all timelines, why do I still exist?"

"They erased you across the present when the crime took place. I pulled you from a past."

I held my breath for a moment and then exhaled. "But if I exist in the past, I would just come to commit the same crime again, right?"

"Not exactly. The FBI was already on their way to stop you, remember? That would be the adjusted timeline. Before TIME's intervention, the FBI would've been another couple of hours; the time it took for them to believe what you had accomplished."

"And what about…," I nodded toward the columns.

"Oh, that. I discovered videos of your experiment on the internet. I tried to replicate your gateway in order to find Eve, but I couldn't get it to work. Like I said before, I'm not smart when it comes to those things."

I looked back at the ceiling. "It's a lot. What you're saying. What you're asking for. It's hard to believe. You stopped me before I turned on the machine. For all I know, it started smoking. Maybe if I saw it actually—"

"There wasn't enough time. The uncertainty for traveling that far back was too risky. I could have arrived the moment the FBI did. Or after. Earlier was safer. But you're right. From my perspective, it's been a century and a couple of years. For you, only a moment." Lucifer stood, walked over to the table, and poured another cup. The same powerful aroma refilled the room.

"Drink this," he said, as he returned. "Don't worry, it's not poisoned. See?" He drank some to prove it. "It'll help you adjust to the time change." He leaned forward, tilted the cup toward me, and pressed it against my closed lips.

I didn't move. The rich scent opened my nostrils, but my lips didn't share their enthusiasm.

"Don't be like that," he scoffed. "Once you're feeling better, we'll go outside. You can decide after I show you this future and all its possibilities for love."

B.3 Path of Eden

An enormous wall visible from the streets, like mountains from a valley, nearly encapsulated the view outside the garage walls. To the northeast, seven square columns rose in staggered heights. Their aesthetic suggested a utopian future rather than the dystopia the literary works of my time had depicted. There was no evidence of an apocalyptic event, such as warning signs about the air quality, or a densely populated city because it was one of the few remaining. No tattered flags of a rebellion. No banners with the stern face of a dictator draped on the tallest buildings. And the sky, oh the sky, reflected the world beneath it like a mirror. Wherever I was—whenever I was—it was far more beautiful than the when and where I had come from.

"What is this place?" I spun in circles, my head tilted back to admire the view.

"We'll call it Eden."

"You're really sticking to the biblical theme, aren't you?"

Lucifer shrugged. "It works. The surface is paradise for the 'angels', a.k.a. model citizens. If one commits a crime, they're thrown to Earth, which is everything below the surface." Lucifer stroked his chin. "Hmm, the reference works a little too well, actually."

"There's a below? And the sky? How's it doing that?" I pointed upward. If anyone ever thought they were alone in this world, they could look up and see everyone else.

Lucifer thrust his hands in his pockets. "The wall is a mural that projects the image in the sky. Reflections or something like that. It's also a reminder of a world that could be if we don't all get along and take care of it. A world divided. A civilization living above the polluted earth. The dystopian possibilities are endless."

"What's on the other side?"

"The other side is more city, same view, and some idiot asking the same question."

I stared at him in disbelief.

He nodded at the towers. "Then the corporations got involved. Now the wealthy live there. Thousands of condos make up a column with a few neighborhoods atop the…Heavens."

We walked several blocks toward a monorail station coated in the same light blue, gray, and white hues as the other edifices. Digital displays of maps showed the monorails connected to large sectors of the city, and autonomous cars shuttled people within those sectors.

I marveled at everything. Fountains so clear they looked dry. Streets so clean, the birds never descended. Inspirational digital banners aplenty, such as YOUR VOICE MATTERS. And with the lack of engine and city noise, there was an outdoor quiet I had never experienced before. A quiet so profound, I could make out the words of a song a block away.

I said I love you…

It wasn't broadcast from the mounted speakers around the city. The voice was singular, unaided by technology, and came from one direction. No musical instruments accompanied the words I ran toward. In such a peaceful city, I could believe that a woman was singing in the street. Her voice beckoned me as I left a disgruntled Lucifer behind.

They're three simple words, but a whole lot of meaning

A group of people stood in front of a damaged, multi-story building with glass walls. Neither the building's structural state nor the bystanders intrigued me. It was the song coming from beyond the crowd that lured me through them.

They're three simple words that I cannot stop singing
Through morning and mid-day and evening the same

Getting through was easier than I expected. Spectators instinctively moved aside. No shoving. No pushing. Everyone seemed mesmerized by the song.

I cannot stop singing, and your love is to blame

At the front, several men in white tuxedos stood guard with wrists crossed at the belt line. I saw my dark complexion reflected off the glasses of two as they responded to my movement beyond the arc formed by the bystanders.

"Hold your horses, kid," Lucifer said, as he grabbed my shoulder and pulled me back. "That one's way out of your league, and the fine gentlemen standing around her will bury you six feet underground next to your heart."

"Who is she?" I asked, pointing beyond the guards to the woman standing among the debris.

The woman illustrated the song with her arms, gesturing them outward toward the building and then inward toward her chest. A long white dress fanned out from around her calves as she danced in front of the steps.

Never have I felt a high such as this
A moment or two—no, an eternity of bliss
The warmth of your kiss, and the touch of your
hand
Every moment with you was amazing and grand

I nudged Lucifer for an answer as rubble lifted from the ground, untouched. As more pieces moved, I realized they were being stacked in an order—that the building was being reconstructed.

"She would be Camille, I think," Lucifer said.

"You think?" I wondered how anyone could forget such a beautiful voice. I had only heard a couple of verses and felt they were hard-coded into my brain. Then there was the rubble she lifted with her voice or hands. *How was she doing that?*

Lucifer shrugged. "I don't keep up with idols. More than an idol, though, she's a Vocalist. They are, uh...mons—" He mumbled the rest as the song shifted from its cheerful tone to a melancholic one that seemed to touch him.

Never have I fallen from so far up and on high
Lost in confusion, I simply forgot how to fly

The words reached me, too, and the harmony moved me, but something about my behavior must have differed from those around me. The guards fixed their attention on us. And soon after, she did, too.

Camille walked toward us as she sang.

Down to the unfamiliar ground, I was unhinged
My wings thereafter, the feathers, they were all singed

The crowd synchronized their steps with hers; as she drew near, they moved away. Lucifer and I stood still, like idiots. I was more the idiot than he, since he moved but stopped mid-step because of me.

As I lay there shedding the last of my tears
I felt something within me that whisked away all of the fears

The harmony she produced faded as she reached us. The debris stopped moving when she made eye contact. Her irises rivaled the greenery designed to beautify the entrance to the building.

"You're talking," she said.

The remaining debris under her control fell to the ground.

I apologized, the words escaping so fast I wasn't sure which ones I used. I wondered if we had stepped into the middle of a play or film. There were no cameras in sight. No one giving direction. Just her, the men in white, and a captivated group of people.

Camille raised her head toward Lucifer. She pushed a couple of strands of her red locks aside, and a tropical scent blossomed. "Please, finish what you were saying."

For the first time, Lucifer was tight-lipped.

"I insist," Camille added with a smile.

Lucifer cleared his throat, more uncomfortably than out of fear. "Vocalists were originally a government experiment to control people through speech. Hypnosis, or something."

"You mean VoCAl—Voice Control and Alteration?" Camille asked.

"Yeah, see, it's one of those weird acronyms used by the military." Lucifer laughed, like someone shrugging off an embarrassing moment.

"*Vocalists*," Camille emphasized, "were artists who could move others with their music. I guess you could say their presence on a stage evolved over time. The military tried to weaponize it, thus creating VoCAls." She raised both of her hands to her chest. "I am a Vocalist. My voice is natural and a gift from my mother."

I lowered my head, almost bowing. "I'm sorry we were talking during your performance."

Camille lifted my chin. The touch of her fingers cooled the blood that rushed to my head.

"No, please, keep speaking your mind. It's been a long time since anyone could do so during, or immediately after, my performance," she said.

I raised my eyes to hers and asked. "Why? How did you do that to the building?" I expected a snarky comment from Lucifer, but he was still silent.

Camille smiled before genuine laughter unraveled her composure. "The world dances to the rhythm of my songs."

"It was a very beautiful song," I said.

"Why thank you. I wasn't sure, since you seem unaffected."

"What do you mean?"

In a soft voice, Camille sang:

Everything is a molecule propagating through space

She danced toward the left, several steps in slow succession with her rhythm.

Everything is a signal moving at its own pace

She danced back toward the right, gradually skipping faster until she stood in front of us again.

When I touch you, energy is transferred with grace

She guided her right hand along my shoulder as she circled me. The hairs on my arms rose with my chest, and both forgot what it meant to fall.

But since nothing is perfect, not all of the energy is transferred this way

Camille stopped in front of me and said, "I synchronize my songs with the remaining energy propagating through inorganic objects, and my voice causes a collision that sends those objects in the direction opposite that energy." As she slid her hand down from my shoulder to my chest, she continued, "Starting with the strongest response down to the weakest until no energy remains. Their resting place." Her hand stopped at my heart.

She withdrew most of her hand except for one finger and whispered, "Not nearly this much energy, though." She tapped the location of the organ threatening to burst from my chest.

I was speechless, the sound of my heartbeat louder than the thoughts in my head. The ones I struggled to piece together into words and articulate.

Camille winked at me and then stepped back. "Thanks for talking to me...," She waited for the name I stumbled upon.

"Michael." Lucifer said for me.

"I hope we meet again, Michael. Everything has its song, and I hope to hear yours one day. So leave a seat in the front row for yours truly, Camille." She spun around twice and ended a third with her bare back to me while waving farewell.

The guards followed behind her, maintaining a distance of several feet. She crouched to touch a piece of broken glass before they ushered her onward.

"Damn Vocalists," Lucifer muttered. "If we're going to hang out, there need to be some ground rules. Rule number one, no Vocalists." He seemed angry.

"Isn't that kind of discriminatory?"

"There is no discrimination here. No sexism, racism, extremism. Whateverism. We're all equally unequal." Lucifer walked as if direction eluded him.

Then I realized something worse. "Oh no! I lied to her. I mean, it wasn't the first thing out of my mouth, but still. Why did you give her that fake name?"

Lucifer paced back and forth. "We're running from an entity that controls time and you want to use your real name? What if doing so helps them find you?"

"You okay?" I asked. Lucifer's pacing had increased.

"No, I'm not okay. Vocalists mess with your head, your emotions, and who knows what else. I can't—I don't want them messing with my memories of Eve."

"I don't think she would—"

"You don't know anything, kid. She's using signals to disrupt other signals. I don't care who you are, you can't completely control that shit." Lucifer took deep breaths until he regained his composure. "Everything outside the primary direction of a Vocalist's voice is subject to side effects. I don't remember exactly what hers does, but you can see the effect it has on people." Lucifer gestured toward the crowd that had dispersed in mild confusion.

"Why didn't it affect me?"

"Because you haven't been here the last hundred years. Some genius discovered chemicals that enhanced the effect Vocalists have on stuff. He sold it to the government, who then created VoCAls. They're a special division of the police who use voice commands to control people.

"Infringement of something or other, right? You'd think? But the people of Eden voted for that shit. They opted in. 'If you have nothing to hide, then it won't hurt you' is the turd they stamped their signatures with. So the government put those chemicals in the water supply to enhance vocal effectiveness on people. They also added the chemical to building supplies used for government facilities. Your beloved Camille makes a fortune repairing damaged buildings."

"So this was a government building? I wonder what happened to it. Domestic terrorism?"

"Nah, some adoptee must've lost their cool, and their head, in an extravagant way."

I remained silent. I couldn't decide which was crazier: Lucifer's plan to fight an extratemporal entity, people's heads blowing off, or Vocalists.

While I thought about it, Lucifer rambled on. "I stopped drinking the water years ago, traveling back in time to get bottled water, but apparently, it ain't all out of my system."

Ignoring his woes, I focused on Camille. "I bet we interrupted her work. I hope she didn't get in trouble or fired."

Lucifer shook his head. "Fired? Those man dolls make sure she never quits. She's a princess locked in the tower of her own voice."

"What are you saying? She's a prisoner? We should help her!" I said with enthusiasm and then finished in a less enthusiastic tone, "She hid her suffering so well behind that electric smile."

"Don't get all poetic on me. Eve comes first. I don't care what you do after that. Keep in mind that not every distressed damsel needs saving. In fact, she probably lives comfortably atop one of those columns." Lucifer glared at the wall with contempt.

"Let's save Eve, then. Where do we start?"

Lucifer greeted my newfound purpose with a mischievous smile. From his pocket, he pulled out a crumpled piece of paper. "First, we go shopping."

I rotated and flipped the paper until the words were upright. The handwriting was one thing, but the contents were in a league of their own.

something crystal
amplifier
something IC
24 awg
faith
love

I blinked several times. "This list sucks."

Lucifer snatched it from me. "Eve made this list, and she's eight billion times smarter than you. Moron."

I apologized and then asked, "But seriously, how do you know what anything is?"

"You leave that to me. Your job is to figure out how to use them after I get them."

I nodded and held back questions about using faith or love. "Where to first?"

Lucifer's grin was almost sinister. "Karaoke."

B.4 Path of Earth

A large, colorful neon sign read: KARAOKE, and in smaller font above it: DESIGNATION 0018. The sign flashed various combinations of blue, pink, green, yellow, and purple to be the brightest spot on the block.

The interior resembled a repurposed movie theater. Multiple corridors branched from the main lobby into hallways that led to individual outlets with unique titles, followed by a time. Below each sign was a teenager wearing clothes with large, custom lettering enhanced by the same neon colors as the entrance.

After declining an offer for refreshments, I followed Lucifer down one hallway. We passed several outlets with titles such as ALPHABET SOUP and SOULARIS until we reached SIREN, the one at the very back. Lucifer exchanged words with the teenager manning the station, who was reluctant to hand me a ticket from his roll.

Inside, the room opened up to a building on the surface, a view that clarified the difference between the two worlds Lucifer claimed were unequally equal.

Above, the people of Eden dined at fancy tables covered with white cloths, illuminated by chandeliers composed of daylight LEDs, and brought to life by casual conversations and laughter.

Below, the people crammed into metal bleachers, shoulder to shoulder, in a dimly lit auditorium that violated every fire code of my time. They unwrapped processed foods with savory scents and clutched plastic cups as they shouted and cheered at a man and a woman standing at the center of the stage.

The man on stage held the microphone with confidence and mumbled aloud:

Look, I ain't always the life of the party
I'm a be honest
But I'm the life of this shorty
I put my sanity on it

Unimpressed, I turned to Lucifer. "So, why are we here again?"

"*I'm* here to find this crystal thingy. It's black-market stuff, and the guy who sells it loves to hang out here." Lucifer weaved his way through the crowd. Without his flamboyant gait, I might've lost him.

The sudden cheer of the crowd startled me. The male competitor held both arms up as he demanded more recognition from the audience.

Lucifer stopped in a less crowded area of the theater. "Your job is to recruit *her*." He nodded toward the woman taking hold of the microphone.

A colorful announcer with black, gelled hair curled upward in the back to match his tailcoat spoke over the rowdiness. "That was Keep the Change putting his sanity on the line! Let's see how Siren responds to his proclamation!" The crowd erupted with excitement.

I was less enthused. "Um, exactly how am I supposed to do that?"

"Beat her in a rap battle. That's your thing, isn't it? Ignore the fact that she's undefeated with an impressive win streak of some hundred or so. That'll only demoralize you. If you win, she'll do whatever you want. Might even marry you."

I stepped in front of Lucifer. He could've knocked me over with his step, but avoided the collision. "I'm not trying to win a girl through cheesy rap battles," I said.

"I'm offended. No, *they're* offended," Lucifer mocked. "This place is an opportunity for convicts to earn freedom in some form or another. Every win is time off their sentence. If they lose, they serve the rest of that time in someone else's care. It's entirely optional, and there are rules and laws in place to ensure the safety of all those involved." Lucifer rattled off the information like a public service announcement. "I wouldn't wish the consequences of breaking those laws on my worst enemies. Except TIME. Obviously."

After a moment of reflection, I felt guilty about calling the rap battles cheesy.

Lucifer placed a hand on my shoulder. "I didn't say you had to marry her. But when I look at you, I see a guy who needs a strong woman in his life. You've been chasing flowers in the wind for too long. It's time to pick one up off the ground. She might be a little rough around the edges, lost a petal or two, but with thorns like hers, people will think twice before stepping on her."

"That's your pep talk?"

Lucifer gave me a thumbs up with his other hand. "I believe in you!"

I turned back to the stage. Siren invaded her opponent's personal space, as did her saliva, which was the closest to kissing her full lips that he'd ever be.

If I could have your attention, please
You're guilty of a ten-minute turn on 2nd street
I live life in the fast lane
Doin' fifty 'round the curve just to hear my tires screech

She was energetic. Her mixed racial background contributed to the head full of curls that swayed with her words. Like Camille, she used her hands for emphasis, and occasionally, she turned to the crowd to immerse them. If adding her to his entourage was part of Keep's plan, then she shredded it to pieces in front of him.

You're in the way of my daily high
Keepin' all the lights from blurring as I pass them by
Behind the wheel is a life in ecstasy
But you're bringin' me down to earth like the devil from the sky

I watched the light fade from Keep's eyes as he walked away empty-handed. The winner was determined by the rowdiness of the crowd, and they never gave the announcer an opportunity to gauge Keep's performance. They never settled down after Siren's name was called.

"I don't stand a chance," I said. To myself, since Lucifer was long gone. I wasn't worried about being lost. He needed me, which was a strange feeling. Nobody had ever needed me before. I also knew that if he could find me in the past, he could find me in another place I didn't belong. Lucifer had dressed for the occasion, and his style was consistent with the spectators. He wore jeans and a fitted, untucked, button-down shirt. I stood out with khaki cargo pants and a long-sleeve tee. What I wasn't certain of was whether I could complete his request. I had never stood onstage without starting a tab first.

The announcer silenced the crowd, and the thousands of LEDs comprising his tuxedo waned. "My friends! This next battle is special. This will be Siren's 150th battle! It's unheard of—wow! Whoo! Yeah!" The crowd cheered until the announcer settled them down again.

With an excessive flair, he pulled out a small piece of paper. "Let's see who'll be lucky number 150." After reading the name to himself, he exclaimed louder than the crowd, "We have an archangel!" He jumped up and down and pumped his fist into the air with excitement. His tuxedo shimmered brighter, its intensity tied to his energy.

"Remember the Archangel Adam who left our Eve speechless after fifty straight wins? We never had another quite like him. A few copycats, yes."

The audience booed.

"Now, I can tell you—no, I can assure you—this one is genuine. Whether he lives up to the name, the predecessor, or you lovely people's expectations, I don't know. But let's give it up for the Archangel Michael! Yeah! Yeah!"

"No, no," I mumbled as I stepped backwards, cursing Lucifer's name as if it wasn't already. He'd signed me up against a reigning champion, and expectations for my performance nearly brought the building down.

The numbers on the ticket I held flashed a bright white through my fist, and a spotlight shone over me. Every pair of eyes turned to me. Running wasn't an option. I doubted the crowd would part as peacefully as Camille's, but I was sure their laughter would follow me up to Eden.

The glass panels muted any excitement or disappointment from above, and likewise, the bustling crowd below. As Eden silently judged me, every hesitation I showed, every fear I allowed to be visible, would impact the bets they probably placed.

"Michael! Come on up!" The announcer waved at me with enthusiasm. The passion in his eyes was difficult to ignore.

My legs moved on their own. The eyes above followed me. The crowd shouted my name, patted me on the back, and cheered me onward. I trudged up the steps and onto the stage, where I saw Siren from a new angle. She was gorgeous, with a soft, hardened face. Amber eyes that matched the highlights of her hair stared me down. The rise and fall of her chest caused her bare cleavage, glistening with sweat from her recent victory, to captivate my eyes. She noticed. The announcer noticed, and then he informed the crowd.

"Michael, keep your eyes on the prize—and I mean her lips," he nudged me. The theater lost its cool once again. "They have crushed many a soul whose eyes wandered far too low. If you don't listen to what she has to say, at your expense, she'll make you a fool fo sho."

Impossible. All of it. Averting my gaze. Winning the battle. Walking away with my dignity intact. I was on a fool's errand.

"Let's get this show started!" the announcer shouted in an obnoxious tone. "Wait, wait, we got to make this one special. We need to make sure history… Remembers. This. Battle! So, instead of two verses each, they'll get three! You heard it! Three! Count it for me!"

The crowd responded in unison, "One, two, three!"

"Yeah! Now, three, two, one, Siren!"

Siren didn't hesitate. The second the mic touched her hand, the words that will be inscribed on my tomb began digging my grave.

The uncharted, undiscovered idiocrasy
Of the self-proclaimed man standin' right in front of me
Always talkin' and lookin' down at me
As if he were somethin' for all the world to see

Now he's crying like I'm supposed to feel sorry for his story
The way I used to when I held him tight and said he never had to worry
The same words that are clear now used to be blurry

So much that I felt like I was reading my own god-damn story

And while I thought I was in love with him, he's not my happy ever after
Goals, morals, and love don't mean the same—there's a lot of different things we're after
But it's about time we flipped to the last page of this chapter
The one followed by a good place full of love and stomach-hurting laughter

"Oh. My. God. Siren! Leave the man with some dignity! Baby girl is moving on!" The announcer clapped with both hands outward as he ran about the stage and egged the crowd on. They cheered for what felt like an eternity. I should have put some words together, but my morale was further ground into the dirt.

The announcer handed me the microphone. I grabbed it but never felt it. I stood in silence for a good minute before his voice surrounded me again.

"Oh no! Could this be the fall of the Archangels?" The announcer danced around me.

It wasn't long before the crowd got involved. "It's why he's single! Loser! Get off the stage!"

My pride was being stoned. Their words hit me like rocks until one awakened a memory buried long ago. And with its revival, emotions I had sealed for a reason. I clenched the microphone in my hand, gritted my teeth, and stepped forward.

I just can't believe, I spent so much time on my knees

For you I'd do anything to please, for you I'd move the mountains from their deeds
And all this time I thought that we were planting seeds, you were growing weeds
And poisoning the foundation I laid to meet your every need

The laws of physics I planned to bend in hopes that I could mend
The lies you strive to defend when really you just want it all to end
I hope one day you'll understand, the pain I desperately tried to fend
Off on my knees with hallelujah and Amen

Time to analyze the information
Time to change the god-forsaken station
And the lyrics comprised to make up my indoctrination
After the last chapter, a revelation
That maybe I could live this life without the presentation
Of your soul that is your infestation

The words took flight. An empty nest remained after the chirping ended. The crowd was as silent as the sky I'd leapt toward. They were my wings. Whether I flew or fell was up to them. To my surprise, nobody laughed. Nobody insulted me. A man in Eden smacked a wine glass off his table and stormed off.

At last, the announcer broke the silence. "We have a winner," he whispered. His voice rose. "History continues to write about this day! We have a winner!" The crowd remained silent. "Stories tell the tale of the man who left a woman speechless. Today, we have the man who left the world speechless! Your winner is… the Archangel Michael!"

The audience cheered on cue. They whistled, applauded, and even stood.

Siren objected. "No! No, there was no rhythm in that! He was talking!"

The audience ignored her plea, but Siren interrupted the celebration anyway after she grabbed me by the collar and yanked me toward her. "You cheated," she whispered loudly. "Are you a Vocalist?"

I shook my head.

"Concede." After a moment of silence, she pulled me closer. "I said, con—" She dropped me. Muffled sounds of pain escaped her as she grabbed a band around her neck. I hadn't noticed it before. Maybe if I had looked up.

The announcer crouched beside her, held the microphone away from his mouth, and placed a hand on her back. "Siren, I understand your pain. The sharp pain of defeat. The greater pain of this system." He lowered his eyes and frowned. "I'm part of it, too. I haven't seen daylight for years. But you have a chance—a better chance than most in your position will ever have." He made eye contact with Siren. "You gotta walk out with your head held high, so that those watching will have hope."

"I don't care about their hope. I want my fucking freedom!"

The announcer whispered, "I don't want to see you end up like... With your sentence, you'd have to win hundreds more. And with the bets always placed on you, it's only a matter of time before someone arranges your defeat. Who knows who you'd end up with then?

"Look at the bright side, love." He looked at me without a shred of disdain in his eyes. "If he's anything like Adam, I know you'll be in the care of someone wonderful."

Siren's clenched fist loosened. She stood up, head still down, a salty expression on her face, and tears dripping from her cheeks. The crowd's applause was respectful as she walked past me without a glance.

The announcer extended a hand toward me and said in the plainest voice I had heard from him all night, "Please, take care of her."

After helping me to my feet, he raised the microphone to his mouth and reprised his role. The energy in his voice returned, lifting the audience's mood with it, as he introduced the next competitors.

B.5 Path of Uriel

A victory should have felt better. After all, I had won a rap battle. I had also won another person's life, which wasn't the prize you walked away with at the county fair. And if for a second I thought it was all a joke, the metal band around her neck reminded me.

Siren stood by the garage's side door with arms crossed. She was quiet, but her body language shouted obscenities. A body as fit as her curves allowed. A rage that hadn't wavered since we'd left Karaoke. Twice she'd asked about my connection to Adam and why I had taken part without knowing what winning meant. I'd assured her that answers were on the way. If she discovered my victory was a fluke, she'd probably kill me. Or so I thought. A website detailing our new relationship showed otherwise.

"Welcome to the Convict Adoption and Rehabilitation Program of Earth, Department of Immigration and Emancipation Management," I read aloud from one of Lucifer's computers. His cyber security practices were terrible. Eve was the username, and he omitted the password.

"CARPE is a program designed to give convicts serving life sentences a chance to live outside of prison. Most can be purchased for a flat fee, but others can be attained through events put on by DIEM. The program was designed to reduce incarceration numbers and minimize the cost of correctional facilities." I stopped reading. Siren's glare pricked the back of my neck.

"Life sentences? What did you do?" I asked.

No response.

I continued reading. "As an adopter, you are partially responsible for any laws the adoptee breaks while in your care. To dissuade such behavior, a Voice-Activated Collar, or VAC, is programmed to respond to the adopter's vocal commands. Ignored commands will cause the VAC to vibrate. Repeated offenses will trigger electrical shock (indicated by a flashing blue light), increasing (indicated by multiple blue lights) with each act of insubordination until the adoptee complies or the adoptee is incapable of responding. Verifiable crimes committed against the adoptee by the adopter will result in the adopter receiving the full sentence of the adoptee regardless of time remaining." That explained the consequences Lucifer had mentioned earlier.

I scrolled down. "There is a maximum time for vocal recognition of the adopter that must be observed. If the VAC doesn't recognize the adopter's voice within the specified time, the VAC will end the life of the adoptee." I paused, disturbed by the consequence of death. I glanced at Siren, who stood like a statue with eyes closed.

"The default time is twenty-four hours. This time limit can be reduced to twelve hours and extended to forty-eight hours." As I skimmed the page, one section caught my attention, which I read to myself.

"The VAC reacts to the aggression of the adoptee, which helps discourage the adoptee from causing physical injury to the adopter. It should be noted that the VAC does not end the adoptee's life immediately. Death of the adopter is possible if the adoptee can withstand the initial and increasing electrical shocks. However, if vocal commands to stop are registered by the VAC prior to the adopter's death, the VAC will trigger and end the life of the adoptee."

As if on cue, Siren asked, "What does it say about the accidental death of the adopter?"

I ignored her sly remark and turned away from the accompanying smirk. But I watched her from the corner of my eye. She was a convict serving multiple life sentences, but she didn't seem like a bad person until I opened my mouth. "Not like I wanted—"

"Then why did you do it? I had a plan! You ruined any chance of me erasing my sentence. There are no reductions to your sentence once you're an adoptee. I'm screwed! Stuck with you till the day I die, you piece of—"

"Because I asked him to." Lucifer walked in the door beside her. "Glad to see everyone getting along. One big happy—"

Siren grabbed him in a chokehold. Her muscles flexed as she tightened her arm around his neck. Lucifer's height forced her to hold him at an awkward angle, but her lower center of gravity, combined with her astonishing strength, made escape impossible.

"Siren, let him go." The VAC around her neck vibrated once. When she refused to let go, a blue light on the collar flashed, and an electrical shock raised the veins along her neck.

"I'll kill him!" she shouted. A second light on the collar flashed. Then a third. "Dammit! Dammit!" She threw Lucifer to the ground and collapsed beside him.

Lucifer got up first, cursing.

I grabbed him before he could follow through with a well-aimed kick. "It's over. It's over!" I pushed him aside and waited for both of them to calm down. "Were you really going to kick a defenseless woman?"

Lucifer massaged his neck. "Man, woman, or child. Like I said before, we're all unequally unequal. Or something." He stumbled farther into the room.

I walked up to and knelt by Siren. "Are you okay?"

She raised her head. Red eyes narrowed and glared at me. Then she spit in my face.

I wiped my face with my sleeve. "You owe us an explanation!" I shouted at Lucifer. "Why did I adopt her? Why didn't you tell me about the VAC program?"

Lucifer tilted his frown toward me. "We are the archangels Lucifer, Michael, and Uriel." He pointed to himself, then to me, and Siren last. "Our goal is to defy TIME—the Temporal Interdimensional Multi-dimensional—" Lucifer paused after I raised my hand. "Seriously, kid?"

I asked anyway. "Why is she Uriel?"

Lucifer sighed. "You honestly think Siren is her real name? It's a stage name and not an archangel."

"Was Adam your stage name? He's not an arch-angel either, right?"

"What's really bothering you, kid? You want to know her real name?" Lucifer mocked. "Well, that brings me to rule number one: no real names. The enemy can't get from us what we don't know. I recruited you two to help me rescue the love of my life, Eve. Michael is going to build me a spatial thingy to help me find and reach Eve. Uriel is going to help me fight TIME and anyone who gets in my way. In return, I am helping Michael find the love of his life—"

Siren laughed from the ground. "I knew it. Eden's men are all the same, or a short fall from the garbage atop the wall. Did you sign this kid up thinking I'd become his? I'll never love him. And if he ever touches me, I will break him, even if it kills me."

My heart skipped several beats. "I don't plan on doing any of that," I said.

Lucifer stepped closer to Siren, but maintained a safe distance. "Michael might be able to get that thing off your neck."

Siren's eyes widened.

Lucifer continued, "He's a genius. He built a spatial gateway that sucked his world into oblivion. I think he can manage a little necklace made by the lowest bidder. Nobody's going to force you to love him, but I hope you can pretend. Some women love a man who is already taken."

I shook my head at her. *You don't have to pretend either*, I mouthed.

"So now that we're all on the same page, can we pretend to be one big, happy family?" Lucifer asked, arms open for a rhetorical hug.

Siren laughed in disbelief. "This is some... Are you guys on drugs? If I could have some of that, I might just believe you." She looked around the room, at the array of monitors and the gateway components, and laughed some more. "You guys think you're in some secret spy movie? Vigilantes—"

Lucifer stuffed a piece of bread into Uriel's mouth. I never saw him move, only a brief afterimage of where he'd started. He must have used the temporal modulator—the name I gave his time-manipulating vambrace. He'd used it to tell his story yesterday by adjusting the time it took his words to reach me. A similar application could explain how he closed the distance to Siren in an instant and how he planned to fight TIME.

"You got the drop on me before. Now we're even." Lucifer winked at her and then walked toward the desk. "Let's get down to business." He grabbed a small object off the desk and tossed it at me. It floated toward me in slow motion and dropped into my hands at normal speed.

He said, "A crystal like that is in my bracelet. I don't know what it does, but I spent the rest of my life's savings on it. Educate me. You know, high level."

I twirled the crystal in my hands. It was transparent and didn't magnify or distort objects viewed through it. "I'll have to do some research. Do you know what it's called?"

"No idea."

I walked up to the desk, sat in the chair, and stroked the keys. After several minutes of producing the only sound in the room, I found some information.

"It's a man-made crystal called the one-way diamond, or power crystal. Each facet is a one-way mirror. If energy is pushed into the diamond, it acts like a capacitor, storing and amplifying up to gigawatts' worth of energy. Whoa!" I stood, excited. "Instead of drawing continuous power from a source like my neighborhood power pole, the temporal modulator stores energy in the power crystal and discharges as required. But that much energy… If used incorrectly, this thing could explode."

Nobody shared my enthusiasm.

Lucifer blinked at me.

Uriel complained, "I'm hungry."

Lucifer clapped his hands. "I leave it to you, kid. Don't blow me up. Make yourselves at home. There are some delicacies in the fridge upstairs. I'll go pick up this A W G stuff."

"American Wire Gauge," I said. "It denotes electrical wire sizes."

Lucifer shot me a sharp glance. He opened the door and added, "Oh, and try not to go outside without me. Earth doesn't care about who you are, but Eden will." He closed the door.

Uriel stormed past me and ran up the stairs like she didn't want to be in the same room as me. I didn't mind. I was used to being alone in the garage. In the house, really.

For a moment, we were like a family. A dysfunctional one. Not exactly the kind I envisioned, which was one dream I was determined to hold on to. A dream where I would hear some other noise in the house every once in a while. A wife wrestling with a hobby. A kid imitating sci-fi television shows.

Then I heard it through the ceiling.

"How the fuck is frozen pizza a delicacy?"

The following days were quiet. Lucifer ran errands for components and tools. Most notably, a roll-up tablet similar to the one on his left arm. Eve had affixed the paper-thin computer to a metal arm brace, added some insulation in between, and integrated the ancillary components, including the power crystal. Then she'd written the program that controlled them. Familiar territory.

Meanwhile, Uriel made herself more at home, which included sitting by the door and startling Lucifer every time he entered, or staring at me while I worked. Not the same menacing glare as when I'd adopted her, but a gradually less intense one.

"Is it true?" she asked while I was researching the protocols of the VAC to incorporate its voice control features into the spatial modulator. "Is what Lucifer said about your world true?"

Smiling because she had spoken to me at last, I lifted the tip of my soldering iron from the circuit. The speech interpreter chip was fragile, and I didn't want to damage it from lack of focus because a woman spoke to me.

"Don't stop what you're doing. I'm not trying to be friends."

Uriel played skeet with my emotions.

"I'm just making noise because it's god-awful quiet in here all the time."

I turned back to the circuit. "There's a high-definition immersive TV upstairs."

Uriel said, "Win her through Karaoke and she'll be yours. Was that your wingman's story to get you laid?"

Irritated, I responded, "I don't know. Lucifer stopped me before I did it—that. I also don't know what runs through his head. I'm looking for something real."

"Eh?" Uriel rested her chin on her raised left knee and extended her right leg outward, bare against the chilled concrete floor.

"And what about you?" I asked. "What did you do for multiple life sentences?"

"None of your business," she said in a teasing tone.

From the corner of my eye, I saw her look away. I sighed. "That's hardly fair."

She shrugged. "Life's not fair."

"Life is fair to all living creatures. Those creatures choose to be or not to be fair to other creatures."

Uriel raised her right knee to the height of her left and leaned back against the wall. "How noble, and deep. Like your lyrics. Did you write those yourself? Once Karaoke finds out you stole some no-name rapper's lyrics, you'll get a collar, too."

I didn't respond. Siren was trying to get under my skin. I wouldn't tell her I wrote those words some time ago—however many years into the future Lucifer brought me—after a woman broke my heart. There was no way to prove that, anyway. There was, however, the possibility that I had risen to fame after disappearing from my space-time, and some actual artist had adopted my lyrics. That would be awesome and a tragedy, according to Uriel.

"Archangel Michael. I think I get it now." Siren smirked. "Cheesy, but cute."

I blew across the circuit board, clearing residual solder from the components.

She continued, "Who is Uriel?"

"No idea."

"That explains why you're single."

I waited for an explanation, doubting that my ignorance of archangels made me unattractive.

Uriel usually made solid eye contact when she spoke, but when I looked at her, she canvassed the room instead, even though nothing had changed since she'd arrived. She was toying with me. Purposely making me wait.

Just as the follow-up question sat on the tip of my tongue, she explained. "I said the name Michael describes you well. Being dubbed Uriel, I asked you about the name because maybe it described me. Maybe I wanted you to learn something about me."

I was speechless, aside from the automatic apology.

"Don't apologize," Uriel scoffed. "You didn't hurt my feelings. Some other girl, though, probably. She'd definitely shut down."

Several memories of similar events surfaced while I sat dumbfounded. All of them showed love interests walking away because I couldn't read their minds. It was frustrating.

"Clock's ticking, archangel. Tick. Tock."

"What? What do you mean?" I raised my hands in frustration, wondering what more there was to do.

"She's walking away."

"What am I supposed to do? I apologized," I said, as if the imaginary woman Uriel had created for the exercise was really walking away.

"Pretty sure I wouldn't be here if an apology fixed anything. Ever. Mister Philosophical doesn't know that actions speak louder than words? You're hopeless. Now Lucifer, he has promise."

Don't panic. Think. Think! I took a deep breath.

Uriel's goal became obvious. I swerved in the seat and rolled myself further down the table to the computer. My fingers glided across the keys until I found the answer she was looking for.

"Uriel is one of the top four archangels, primarily representing wisdom. He helps humans make the right decision between good and evil. A problem solver." I leaned back in the seat. "Why did you do that?"

Uriel shrugged her shoulders. She continued to study the walls and then looked at me. "I'm your pretend girl, right?"

"I don't need a fake lover," I growled.

"No? But maybe Michael does." Uriel stood and stretched, breaking my concentration with her movement, and with a sex appeal of which she was either ignorant or fully aware. She lowered her arms and adjusted the straps of her tank top. "I've been watching Lucifer for the past couple of days. He comes at the right time and leaves at the right time. When you're ready for the next part, he's there with it in hand. Almost like he's done all this before." Uriel looked pensive for a moment. She walked toward me. "Anyway, he doesn't seem the type to do something without a reason. You both act like you're vigilantes in some thriller movie. Maybe we'll infiltrate an event like a charity or a ball. Who knows, maybe you'll get to walk arm in arm with me." She caressed my head as she passed by. "But if you embarrass me like our pretend girl just now, I'll knock you on your ass," she said with a wicked smile.

I spun in the seat as she walked away. "So, you're going to be nice to me now? Or is that pretend, too?"

"I'm doing what I have to do. Whether it's real, I don't know. Sometimes I dream with my eyes open."

She took several more steps and added, "You should live in the moment sometime." She left the garage to its usual silence.

I was relieved. Her presence was inescapable. She even commanded the room when she was quiet. When I thought the distraction was gone, I heard the shower, which wasn't unusual. Uriel singing in the shower—that was unusual.

I believe, we can shine, brighter than the stars in the sky
I believe, we can make, a better world out of all this ice
Warm all the things that weigh us down
And shape the future with our eyes
Just you and me, against the world
We'll make a place for you and I

Focusing on soldering was impossible. Uriel's voice calmed me into an unproductive state. I thought Raphael was the archangel known for healing the mind and the heart. Whatever stress I'd felt from our earlier exchange was gone.

A place for you and I
A place for you and I...I...I...I...
For you and I...
For you and I...I...I...I...

Her voice echoed off the bathroom walls like a harmonious choir. As her pitch went higher and the notes held longer, something stirred within me. A sense of power, as if I was untouchable. It came. It went.

The sweeter side of Uriel's voice rang down the stairs as she skipped several steps to reach the garage floor. "Hey, you hungry?" she asked. After a moment of silence from me, she retreated up a step, looking embarrassed. "Why are you looking at me like that?"

"Your singing just now. It felt…" I searched my head for a logical explanation. "What was that? Are you a—"

"A what?" Lucifer asked. I hadn't heard him come in.

"A professional cook," I said, substituting the word Vocalist because Lucifer hated them.

"Sounds like you two are getting along well." Lucifer smirked and winked at me. "I'd love some of that professional cooking, if I'm worthy."

Uriel slouched against the wall and crossed her arms. She raised a brow. "I didn't know you ate anything outside the frozen aisle."

"I eat frozen foods or gourmet meals. There is no in-between. And here's the gourmet food." Lucifer held up a fancy invitation emblazoned with calligraphy and sprinkled with diamond-like shavings within a gold border. He dropped the invitation into my lap. "You are cordially invited to the Starlight Rooftop Ball hosted by Douglas Winterstorm. Bring your star as we celebrate the brightest in the night's sky and blah blah blah."

Uriel winked at me, and I rolled my eyes.

"Ahem," Lucifer sounded. And then louder, "Ahem!" When our confused silence continued, he said in a disappointed tone, "This is where you ask Uriel to be your date."

I fumbled the invitation in my hand, stood, and turned toward two brown eyes that looked away. "Uriel…"

"You've got a long way to go, kid," Lucifer said, patting me on the back.

"I wasn't ready."

"Nobody's ever ready. Love is a dance where you think on your feet." Lucifer tossed a bag toward Uriel. "Your gown for the evening. Try not to steal the show too much."

I didn't say it, but Lucifer and Uriel were better suited for the event than I. Their model-like appearance reminded me of another place I didn't belong— a place among the beautiful.

"Doug lives in the third to last column," Lucifer said. He pulled out a familiar crumpled piece of paper. "The party will be at the neighborhood town center at the top. I need you to keep tabs on Dougy boy while I find the amplifier. It's an ancient artifact of your time." He nodded at me. "Doug is a collector and keeps his valuables locked in a vault."

"You're going to steal it?" I asked.

"Yeah," Lucifer said, matter-of-fact. "I'll either slow the vault's mechanisms down or teleport inside."

"It's... It's not a teleporter." The technology of this era had helped me, but it was Eve's temporal version that had made replicating the spatial gateway into such a small device possible. Without it as an example, I would've been lost. "I haven't tested it yet. Without the amplifier, there might not be enough power—"

Lucifer motioned for me to hand over the modulator. "Faith, remember?" He tapped the word on his list. "I'm about to steal from one of Heaven's most influential to fight an entity that controls time. A crossed wire or two is the least of my concerns."

Valid point.

"Just make sure the amplifier is plug-and-play." Lucifer snapped the vambrace around his right arm and secured the latches. "How many times can I activate it?" he asked, as he navigated the menus.

I'd copied the user interface of Eve's temporal modulator. Instead of a time down to the millisecond, the spatial modulator required entering a position down to the millimeter. When engaged, it discharged the energy stored in the power crystal to tear a hole in space.

The triangular relationship between energy, distance, and duration constrained the system. The amount of energy discharged determined the distance traveled and how long the gateway remained open. I kept the explanation simple for Lucifer. "The farther you go, the more power is required. It'll take several hours to recharge the power crystal."

Lucifer faced us, both sleeves rolled up and both modulators visible. "Archangels, to the Heavens!"

B.6 Path of Heavens

The town center atop the pillar was a garden of flowered grass that flanked cobblestone walkways. Chandeliers hung from lamp posts, the diamonds dangling from them flickering like stars.

"It's beautiful." Uriel smiled. She had discarded the hair and facial products Lucifer had purchased, preferring a natural look that challenged the scenic view she complimented. The rest hid beneath a long black cloak with violet fur trim across the bottom.

A black suit with a matching vest made my violet shirt and handkerchief pop. Feeling more confident than usual, I reached for Uriel's hand. "May I have this dance?"

Her smile widened. "I'd like that."

I escorted her to the edge of a large section of wood opposite a pianist. Before we left the grass, she pushed the button that fastened her cloak together. It slipped off of her shoulders. She caught it by the collar with her other hand and twirled it around and over her arm.

Beneath the cloak was a knee-length, royal violet dress that shaped her curves and bared her arms. The diamonds adorning the dress shimmered like stars against a violet sky. She was the scenic view, an ensemble that took my breath away.

Uriel led us onto the dance floor. Each step she took blessed the ground beneath her. I found my footing, placed one hand on her lower back, and locked the other with hers as we glided toward the center of the dance floor.

"Are you okay?" she asked.

"Yeah. Sorry. I just couldn't find the words to describe how beautiful you look tonight."

She lowered her head toward my chest. "Stop, you're making me blush. Rosy cheeks won't match this dress."

My heart raced on the inside, but I remained calm on the outside and said, "I was living in the moment."

Uriel relaxed in my arms, the gap between our embrace nearly gone. She tried to hide her grin against my chest. "Oh, jeez. I wasn't ready for that."

"You're the one who suggested it. You should take responsibility for your words." Like lyrics of a song, the words rolled off my tongue. I wasn't sure when talking to Uriel had become so easy.

She raised her head and smiled. "Better yet, I'll practice what I preached…." She stood on her toes and stopped short of kissing me. "I think we're drawing more attention than we wanted," she whispered instead.

People were staring in awe. When someone behind us applauded, the onlookers turned away. Uriel secured her hand in mine as we lowered our arms.

"Good evening, Michael." Camille greeted me in a green, strapless bell dress with fall leaves scattered among her red strands. She held a wineglass in one hand. "We meet again. What melody will we play this time? A duet?" She nodded at Uriel.

"Hi Camille. This is my fiancée, Uriel." The lie rolled off my tongue with ease. Uriel had played her part well, and I wanted to match her effort.

Camille didn't hide her gasp, and Uriel crushed my fingers as she veered away, her cheeks rosy.

"Oh. Oh, yes. Congratulations!" Camille's smile seemed forced. "I should've guessed from the way you danced. I've never seen anything like it—sensual but respectful. You two were in a world of your own. Maybe you can show me sometime."

"Nope." Uriel responded with a razor-edged smile.

Camille looked puzzled. "Oh no, I wasn't trying to—"

"Don't care," Uriel said. An awkward silence followed until nearby laughter joined our conversation.

"Good evening, dear." A stout older man kissed the back of Camille's left hand.

I recognized him as Douglas Winterstorm—our target for distraction. He wore the same white suit as his online photos. His graying hair shone for a moment as he kissed the back of Camille's other hand, too. "I still haven't found a star brighter than you." He reached out to brush strands of Camille's hair from her face.

She evaded with a respectful curtsy. "The night is young, father, and stars are billions of miles away. Their light will take time to reach us."

Doug's hand grasped the air before he lowered it to her right shoulder and opened his other arm toward us. "Indeed, it is! Introduce me to your friends. I have not seen such a fine performance as their dance...." His words trailed off as he focused on Uriel.

"Father, this is Michael, the first man to truly hear my song. And this is his fiancée—"

"Siren?" Doug asked. His eyes bulged and then narrowed as he inched his head forward for a better look.

"You know her?" Camille asked.

Doug lowered his welcoming arm. "I spent a small fortune on worthless thugs trying to gain her. Of all the events put on by DIEM, she chose to be a prize in karaoke. Now, she's this man's adoptee? Fiancée? That's preposterous!"

I had forgotten about Uriel's VAC. She didn't hide it. The band blended well with her outfit. I glanced around and noticed that some servers, bouncers, and the occasional arm candy of Heaven's elite had collars, too. Nobody obscured the dim, orange status light.

"I'm nobody's prize," Uriel growled.

Doug faced me. "Michael, was it? I am Douglas Winterstorm."

"Good evening, Mr. Winterstorm. This is a fine event you have put on tonight," I said with my best smile.

He ignored my flattery. "I'll pay you for her."

Uriel's grip tightened. I considered bargaining to buy the time Lucifer needed, but besides it being reprehensible, I remembered Uriel's threat about disrespecting her in public.

"Sir, I respectfully decline."

"Oh, my fine fellow, I wasn't asking." Doug snapped his fingers, and two men, forged from a similar assembly line as Camille's earlier entourage,

hurried to his side. "Transfer her to me. My designation code is DW2495." He pulled out a phone. "I'll
send you one million."

I cringed. Doug was another rival in my path of
love. The type who solved problems with money instead of compassion. "If you'll excuse us." I turned
and pulled Uriel along.

"I will not." Two more of Doug's men stood behind us. They crossed their arms at the waist and
blocked our escape.

"Oh, but you will." A loud voice echoed across
the courtyard.

Nearby conversations stopped, as did the band's
music, which garnered the attention of those farther
away. Lucifer stood in front of us with his full post-
apocalyptic attire. The straps were still empty, but a
firearm sat in the holster at his side.

"Yo," he said with captivating charm as the window behind him collapsed like water filling a hole.

Doug stood wide-eyed. "What in the heavens just
happened?"

"You did it!" I shouted. "It actually works!"

Lucifer grinned. "Was there ever any doubt?" He
waited for the nearby whispers to settle and said,
"Pick the love of your life, kid, and let's go finish
this."

"What?" I asked.

"I brought you to the perfect place. No finer
women in all of Eden than those attending an event
atop the Heavens."

Lucifer was right. Every woman in sight was
beautiful. They radiated intelligence, success, and
showed loving affection to their dates. Even the collared ones exuded a royal ambiance.

I snapped out of my daze. "Your damsel in distress is waiting, remember? I have all the time in the world to find the love of my life."

"Actually, you don't."

A disturbing silence followed. Everyone seemed as confused as I was. Everyone, other than Uriel and I, should have been.

Lucifer took several steps forward. The people near him moved away. "Michael, as I plotted my escape and revenge during my century of imprisonment, my brain found an answer to every question except one: What happens after I save Eve?"

"We go home," I said.

"Home? We had a home. It was thataway." Lucifer pointed toward the west. "TIME took it away from us. So now what? Build a new home for some other entity or organization to destroy?"

I shook my head. "Lucifer, you're making less sense than usual."

He looked toward the west. "The only way to guarantee our happy ever after is to ensure that no one ever comes after us again—me, Eve, you, and the love of your life."

"How do you plan to do that?" I asked.

"By stopping time."

I felt relieved. "Well, yeah. That's the biggest fight ahead of us."

Lucifer shook his head. "No, you don't understand. I'm going to stop...*time*." He let the word sink in before he explained. "I'll destroy the multidimensional entity, take the technology they used to imprison me, and stop the flow of time for everything except us."

Lucifer's plan was more ambitious than simply fighting this otherworldly entity that I still didn't know or believe existed. Deep down, I hoped TIME was Lucifer's mask for some human organization holding Eve prisoner, similar to the titles he gave us and the future he brought me to.

"His crazy just hit a whole new level," Uriel said. I felt her weight shift. Her fingers loosened in mine, ready to break away at any moment and fight.

"What the hell is going on here?" Doug demanded.

"This doesn't concern you," Lucifer snapped. "I'm having an important conversation with my comrade." He glared at Doug, who backed away despite the number of guards around him. Lucifer's grand entrance had demanded respect.

Lucifer took a deep breath. "Michael, even you have to admit my logic is sound. Nobody would die. There'd be no wars, famine, inequalities. My love for Eve will have saved humanity. And nobody will ever again say it was not enough!"

Now I understood where Lucifer's insane idea had taken root. TIME had said his love wasn't enough to stop them. So Lucifer was determined to prove it was strong enough to do much more.

"Is that what this is about? Forget that, man. Let's save Eve and go home." I waved him over, but he didn't move.

Lucifer scratched the back of his neck. "I'd love to discuss it further, but Eve is in a place where time waits for no one. Are you with me, or are you not?"

I lowered my tone. "I'll help you save Eve, but I won't let you stop time."

"That's your final answer?"

I nodded.

Lucifer sighed. He slid his hands into his pockets and then back out. He looked at his feet and rocked them back and forth. His movements continued as if he gave me time to reconsider. We made eye contact again. Then he said, "Uriel, kill Michael."

I couldn't believe what he said. Was he kidding? Bluffing?

"No," Uriel said.

A quick breath escaped my parted lips. "I see what you meant about control over manipulating signals. You must've left part of your brain behind while traversing space."

As I opened my mouth to say more, Uriel's grip tightened. She doubled over, veins surfacing along her neck. The blue light on the VAC flashed. It was discharging.

"Uriel?" I knelt beside her and commanded the VAC. "Turn off! Stop! Ignore command!" My hands trembled near the black collar, but there was no button to push or setting to adjust. "Why isn't it stopping?" I panicked.

Uriel fell into my arms.

"Because you're not her adopter. I am," Lucifer said.

His words hit me like a truck. My arms tensed, and I had to remind myself that Uriel was in them.

Lucifer continued, "You won Uriel for me in the same manner this cretin," he nodded toward Doug, "dispatched his cronies to win her for him. You didn't notice. All you had to do was give her one command. Ah, but you're too nice for your own good."

I raised my head and my voice to Lucifer. "That's not true. I commanded her when she attacked you. I should've let her rip your head off."

Lucifer raised a brow and smirked. "Did you command her? Or was the VAC responding to the aggression of the adoptee against the adopter?"

Uriel fell prone with her fingers around the VAC as a desperate struggle to fight the electricity coursing through her ensued. She wanted to rip it off, but the metal was at least one inch thick.

Frozen in place, unable to refute Lucifer's logic, I resorted to anger. "Turn it off, Lucifer!"

"And deny her love for you? Look at her, Michael. She's choosing to suffer—to die instead of killing you. Your death would have added negligible time to her sentence and saved her life. If that isn't love, I don't know what is." One of Lucifer's modulators chimed. "Looks like it's ready to go again."

"Why would you do this? You have the spatial modulator!"

"Yeah, but I can't have you building another and bringing the cavalry." Lucifer admired the spatial modulator. "Uriel's job was to remove anyone in my way, which unfortunately became you. I didn't think she'd fail, and I would have considered freeing her had she succeeded. Don't take it personally. I didn't know if I could trust you or her. I had my doubts, and with it, contingencies. I assumed you did the same."

I frowned and averted my gaze.

"Michael, Michael, Michael. You might really be the embodiment of that archangel. And I know what you're thinking—I'm truly the devil. But I'm not evil. God and Lucifer both reached out to humanity. God wanted to keep humanity in the dark, and Lucifer wanted to show them the light. Each strived to do what they thought was right, and as a result, humanity labeled one good and the other evil. I hope they won't remember us in the same manner."

It was hard to deny his logic. But he was wrong. Before I could argue with him, he activated the spatial modulator and vanished.

"Somebody, help!" I cried. "Please!" Tears blurred my vision of the pale Uriel in my arms. "Anybody?" I begged. Nobody moved. Even if someone could help, why would they? The enemy was my ally. "Uriel—no, Siren!"

"Aurora. My…real name is…Aurora…" she whispered.

"I'm so sorry. I should have asked instead of playing his stupid game. My name is Kieran." I pulled Aurora into a tight embrace. She stopped struggling, her strength slowly draining, the rest focused on holding my hand.

In the quiet that followed, Camille sang.

I almost can't believe the words you said to me
What once was butterflies now brought to my knees
There's no escapin' this pain in my heart

Error lights illuminated across Aurora's VAC. First orange, then red, flashing rapidly as the passion in Camille's song increased. She directed the words at Aurora, but sang to me.

How I reminisce those words you sang to me
So full of love, how everything was meant to be
The memories are tearin' me apart

Aurora's body relaxed in my arms as a crack formed along the left side of her VAC. I yanked it off, splitting it in two. The back half fell to the ground as I hurled the front half into the grass. Aurora didn't open her eyes, but her breathing was steady.

And how I knew the world would never under-stand
When you said that we could stay as friends
All I had to do was play my part

I saw other VACs failing as well. Relief spread like wildfire as shackles fell to the ground.

Now there's darkness fillin' up my heart and soul
The screamin' voices louder than you'll ever know
I just couldn't get over losin'...you

I looked at Camille's green eyes. "Thank you," I choked, but forced the words through. "Thank you so much."

"Camille!" Doug grabbed her shoulder and yanked her around to face him. "What are you doing?"

Camille pushed his hand aside. "It's time to stop supporting this inhumane program, father."

"I won't let you destroy everything I have built. You were put on a pedestal by me. I made you!"

"What, exactly, did you make?" Camille asked. The frown she had when singing sunk lower.

Doug mumbled something inaudible.

Camille spoke clear as day. "You created a platform that shared words but never the meaning behind them." She looked at me and exhaled through a smile. "It wasn't until I met him I truly understood what it meant to be heard. Michael, thank you for sharing your song."

"Enough of this little shit stealing what's mine," Doug growled. He signaled the guards to detain Aurora, me, and even Camille. They moved toward Camille, but turned to defend her. "What is the meaning of this?" Doug demanded as two other guards secured him from behind.

Camille ignored him and addressed me. "Can Lucifer really stop time? Had I not seen him arrive the way he did, I would have never asked."

"I'm not sure, but I've seen enough to think it's possible."

Camille frowned. "If I'd known, maybe I could have used my voice to stop him."

"How?"

"Everything's a signal. You can do a lot of damage by disrupting it a little." She picked up a fragment of a broken VAC. "It worked with this. Maybe I could have stopped him from teleporting, too." She tossed the piece to the ground.

"It's not a…wait, where did he teleport to?" I stroked my chin. "He wanted the spatial modulator to find and fight TIME. How would he know where to find TIME if he's never had a way to traverse space? Where would he get the coordinates from—oh, no! I'm such an idiot! *I* must have opened the gateway to TIME. There were coordinates on my screen that he could have seen when he turned off the stream. But that would mean I didn't destroy my world or create a new timeline. That would mean Lucifer's from my timeline's future, and since I destroyed everything when the FBI showed up, his only option for a spatial gateway *and* the coordinates was to travel back in time and find me. Dammit! He manipulated me with every word he spoke." I slowed down before my train of thought escaped even me. Everyone stared, which wasn't anything new after I snuck out of me.

"Sorry, it's been a wild week. I think I know where to find him." Then, more to myself. "Except, there's no following him, since he has the only spatial modulator." I paused for a moment. A eureka moment. "Or does he?" I remembered his attempt to build a spatial gateway and hoped he didn't sabotage the thing on his way out.

Camille straightened her shoulders. "So, how do we stop him?"

"I'm going to build my original gateway out of what he started. I'll use the modulator's software to control it. Should take me a couple hours to adjust the code. Then I'm going to follow him. Alone." I shifted my eyes away from Camille's disapproving frown. "It's probably a one-way trip."

"I'm…going with you," Aurora said.

I looked back down. "Are you okay? You're really in no—"

She grabbed me by the collar.

"Not nego…tiable!" She growled.

Camille's smile was sad. "Well, I won't sit in the front row and argue with the one on stage. You should go before more of my father's men get here."

B.7 Path of Evelyn

The power grid in the future exceeded my expectations. Lucifer's prototype gateway was further along than I expected. After my modifications, it maintained an opening long enough for us to pass through. On the bright side, I didn't pull us into a black hole. Instead, I found the true dystopian world.

A pale blue stained everything in sight. A soft white light without a visible source cast subtle shadows that distinguished floors from walls and edges of corridors leading to other rooms. Above, I saw wall space to the extent of my vision. There were no scents or sounds.

"Where are we?" Aurora asked. Her words carried in all directions. "Shit," she whispered aloud.

I turned around in time to see the remnants of the spatial opening as it closed. I had opened it inside an energy wall that fell apart after the portal's collapse. A wave of blue, semi-transparent energy dispersed across a vertical plane. It spread to two of four rectangular posts that formed a cube composed of the same energy.

Aurora walked into the cube to stand in front of a console and a woman suspended in animation. The woman was diving forward, hand outstretched, and reaching for something. Her outfit matched Lucifer's, except for the complete, full-colored patch of a rocket firing over the earth.

"Is she Eve? And is this the temporal prison Lucifer talked about?" I inched my way toward the room and stepped over the threshold.

"The *what* prison?" Aurora asked.

"Lucifer said they imprisoned him temporally. They slowed his entire body, except for his mind. A day for him could be a decade for us. If you can believe what he says," I added after Aurora raised a brow.

"Honestly, I don't know what to believe anymore. Who built this place? Aliens? Gods?"

"Humans," I said. They had suspended the console like the woman—without wires or a pedestal. I didn't understand the symbols reflecting, projecting, or illuminating crisp orange lines until they slid and rotated in various ways to form one word I understood.

"Evelyn."

After I spoke the name, the display vanished, and the suspended woman descended toward me with grace. Her motion sped up as she landed on her left foot and continued forward until her slender arms embraced me. Then she kissed me. It was soft. Passionate. Exhausting. Before Aurora ripped her away from me and shoved her to the ground.

"Oops, my bad." Aurora shrugged.

I touched my lips. "She was draining my strength. Maybe feeding."

"Feeding? Like a vampire?" Aurora asked in a sarcastic tone.

Eve stood. Her gaze passed over us as if her surroundings were far more important. She walked over to the wall on her right and placed her palm against the energy field. A crackling sound accompanied by her moans of pain filled the silence as the wall collapsed into her hand. She inspected her hand as the remaining flickers of energy traveled across her fingertips.

She walked out into the corridor where we had arrived, still ignoring us, and stopped a few meters down the hallway. A frown replaced her emotionless expression as she turned to face a similar energy field. She drove her fingers into the light, which whined as it fell apart. She entered the room for a moment and then meandered further down the corridor.

"Should we be following her?" Aurora asked. Her voice trembled, and she shook in place as Eve walked away. "That girl creeps me out."

I walked into the room Eve had visited. An uneasiness settled in my gut as I stepped over the threshold. The room was empty except for a glass display suspended like the one in Eve's room. I took a deep breath and focused on the new symbols. The lines conspired to tell me words, but in the end, remained illegible.

"What's the plan?" Aurora asked. Her spunk had returned.

I stepped away from the console. "Find Lucifer and punch him into tomorrow." I hid my fears of fighting Lucifer behind a wide grin.

Aurora rolled her eyes and smirked. "Great plan, except we can't get close to him if he's using those bracelets."

I agreed. "It's clear that Lucifer's always been a step ahead of us. It's time that we took the lead."

She grinned. "Well then, lead the way."

I ran down the corridors, shouting Lucifer's name. If anyone was home, they'd have heard me by now. Maybe I'd alerted TIME, which was okay if it meant stopping Lucifer.

From one corridor to the next, one large room to another, I couldn't tell where I was going or where I had already been. I hadn't seen any other occupied cells, but the blurred energy field enclosing each one distorted the transparency in an unusual way. The place felt like home, but it wasn't.

"Lucifer!" I continued, knowing he would show, eventually. Lucifer liked to hear himself talk. I was certain he wouldn't pass up the opportunity to lecture me about my failures, and maybe even ask about my success getting there. And I was right.

His voice bellowed from behind me. "So you let her die," he said.

When I turned around, he wasn't there. My heart raced and deep breaths replaced my steady breathing.

"I suppose the choice wasn't *really* yours to make. Or was it?" Again, the voice came from behind. "You could have killed yourself and rendered the command impossible. But thinking on your feet isn't one of your strengths."

I needed Lucifer to show himself, so I shouted, "I found Eve!"

Lucifer appeared ten feet in front of me, his face expressionless. "Bravo," he said, but he didn't clap.

I needed to push his buttons enough to keep his attention, but not so much that he'd kill me right away. The thought shook me to the core. I never imagined that someone would try to kill me. "I'm surprised you didn't free her. She's suffering, right? Or maybe you couldn't get past the energy field."

Lucifer raised his right arm. "You gave me the means to bypass the temporal wall. Without time or spatial manipulation, it'd take decades, centuries, or even millennia to pass through one. It's the ideal prison."

"But you didn't free her. I see. You were planning to end the world and ask for forgiveness later, which means she wouldn't have agreed with any of this."

"You don't know anything about Eve," he snapped.

I crossed my arms. "So what's stopping you? Couldn't figure out how to use the temporal wall to stop time as planned? That's a shame, considering using things is your only strength."

Lucifer laughed. "Yes, you're right. I should have used you a little more before discarding you, is what I should say, but this show you're putting on is a poor distraction for a cavalry that's not coming. I've already killed TIME. Oh, and I searched the nearby areas, thinking you'd bring VoCAls, but you didn't. You're all alone."

I wasn't expecting that response, or the cavalry mentioned. He didn't bring up Aurora, so I assumed he hadn't found her.

Lucifer threw his arms wide. "It was cinematic. TIME never saw me coming. Literally. Hey, did you know that speed is a function of time? I couldn't understand how TIME beat me before. We had the same power. Truth is, as native manipulators of time, they were faster. But how do we determine speed? By distance traveled. Now, imagine traveling instantaneously. This spatial modulator ignores time—no, makes me faster than time!"

"What have I created?" I meant to ask myself, but spoke aloud.

Lucifer lowered his arms. "Don't you mean unleashed?" He smirked at my bewilderment. "As you have no doubt discovered, you didn't destroy your world. Yet. Instead, the gate you opened led straight to my cell."

His words caused my memories of the unreadable symbols I saw earlier to move again.

"Michael, you freed me. Well, the future you. The one who turned his back on me. But I saw potential in some part of you. So I went back in time to find a more reasonable you."

I took a step back. "That's… That's impossible. That would mean the future was only a few minutes old, but the place you showed me was well beyond that. This place is well beyond that."

"You're assuming I time traveled immediately. I'm not that bright, remember? It took me a while to learn how to charge and use this damn thing." Lucifer waved his left arm. "And even longer to build your failed gateway. Is that how you got here? I should've destroyed it."

"No, no, this isn't my fault!" I clapped both hands against my ears. "*I* didn't free you and *I'm* not responsible for what future me did."

Lucifer clapped his hands once and leaned forward. "Did you really think you could open a hole in space without consequences?"

I knew there'd be consequences, and I was ready to accept them. Until then, I had to stop him. He just didn't know that the cavalry was already here.

Our lives, bound together by the threads we make
A slow dance, with everything in the world at stake
Stitch by stitch, you unraveled me

The song of the Siren echoed into the large room Lucifer and I occupied. He turned around with arms flailing, but couldn't pinpoint its origin. Not even I knew where Aurora's serenade came from. But I knew what her voice was doing to Lucifer. It either inspired or demoralized those in its path and contributed to her legendary karaoke run.

"You brought a goddamn Vocalist!"

Lucifer hated Vocalists, not because they messed with his memories of Eve, as he'd claimed, but because they messed with his ability to modulate time. Aurora was disrupting the surrounding atoms, which made manipulating his own dangerous.

My soul bared out—my heart on the table
You took my breath away and now I'm unable
To live without the warmth of your embrace

Aurora's voice affected me less, since I'd never been exposed to the enhancing agent. I fought against the weight of her words and charged at Lucifer. He caught my hand and spun me around into a chokehold.

"You're a century too fucking early to fight me!" he shouted. I felt his arm shaking, his stance unsteady.

He may have thought I was trying to break away, but I was exactly where I wanted to be. "Let go of me, Nathan!" The jumbled symbols had rearranged themselves to show me his real name. I realized proximity to the name bearer was required when the symbols shifted after Lucifer appeared.

Lucifer drew a sharp breath. "What did you say?"

"I said... Input command. Reboot. Authentication. Whiskey. Tango. Foxtrot!"

Command received.

The singing stopped. Lucifer released me.

Authentication verified.

Initiating system reboot.

Reboot sequence initialized.

Discharging power crystal.

The sudden discharge of energy knocked me several feet away to the ground. Lucifer staggered backward but didn't fall.

"What did you do?" he raged.

"I activated my contingency," I said with pleasure.

"No, not Eve's too!" Lucifer tapped the temporal modulator's display as it went dark.

"Yeah, you both have terrible cyber security practices."

"You messed with Eve... Your little birdie should've kept singing," he growled. "I'm going to lock you in a prison for eternity. But first, I'm going to tear her larynx out in front of you. In slow fucking motion." Lucifer stomped toward me as I scurried backward.

I had nowhere to go and only a couple of minutes before the modulators rebooted. Lucifer would reach me before then. I scrambled to my feet but fell over halfway up, still disoriented from the blast.

Lucifer lunged for my leg, but missed. He succeeded in his second attempt and then dragged me across the room. I kicked and twisted around to break free, but Lucifer's grip was strong.

"Come out, little birdie! I caught a worm for ya. Or a maggot. Do you eat maggots?"

"I eat pretty boys for breakfast!" Aurora dashed out from around the corner on Lucifer's left. She was quick—natural speed with enough strength behind her fist to knock Lucifer on his ass. Aurora pursued. Both swung their fists, blocked with their forearms, and missed each other by inches until Lucifer reached for her curls. Aurora caught both of his wrists. She slid her fingers down to the modulators and tightened her grip.

"No! What are you doing?" Lucifer cried.

Both systems cracked under the pressure. I heard the metals warp, the screens splinter, and the wires short, followed by the clatter of their pieces against the floor.

"You stupid little—"

Aurora struck him in the face. Blood gushed from his nostrils. At last, his pretty face was stained. She grabbed him by the collar and cocked her fist for another swing, but stopped. Not by choice. Everything stopped except my mind, and the woman entering my field of view from the left.

Eve.

Barefoot, she left ephemeral prints on the floor as she walked up to Lucifer. She knelt down next to him, caressed his bloodied locks, and smiled with empathy. She turned to me as everything turned white and mouthed the words: Thank you.

Charlie Timeline

C.1 Path of Michael

"I'm ready," I said. "Project Title: Path of Love. Time: 0055 hours. The initial run will begin at 0100 hours. The first objective is to open and connect two points in space across a distance of ten feet. The second objective is to send an object from one point to the other, unscathed. The third objective is to extend the range of the gateway beyond Earth. I expect the final objective to fail, primarily due to power limitations. I also expect the gateway to maintain an opening for less than a second. However, if I can get a glimpse of some other place—some other world—it will be a success. I have a high-speed camera with a trigger pulse in line with system activation. I can't stream high-speed videos to social media, so you'll have to check it out later."

The comments supported me. Four of the five viewers wished me luck. One viewer, with the username SerialData, seemed excited with fingers crossed and a thumbs-up emoji, followed by a question: "Who's that behind you?"

I turned to face the platform and shoved the chair out from under me as I jumped to my feet. The chair spun and smacked the desk a couple times as it rolled, and caught the attention of a tall man admiring the pillars.

The man tilted his head back and revealed a pale, slender neck. A blue, long-sleeved attire resembling a flight suit—a post-apocalyptic one from space—shrouded the rest of him. Arrays of empty straps covered his arms and legs.

"Yo." He greeted me with sky-blue eyes. His charismatic smile faded as he faced me. "Before you screw up the timeline, I have a proposition for you."

I searched for clues that would explain his arrival. The garage door hadn't opened—the main or the side. The noisy stairs leading to the kitchen spiraled up behind my desk, but I never heard or saw someone walk down.

"Who are you? How did you get in?"

"I was already here. Or was I?" He stood in deep thought before he asked, "Does being *here* only apply to spatial positioning? Does a past tense statement apply to events that happened in the future? Because, from my perspective, I have always been here. So I will already be here." He considered his words a moment longer before he abandoned them.

"Anyway, you mind turning that off?" He nodded toward the stream. "I'm camera shy."

I shook my head. There was no way *he* could be camera shy. With slick, black hair and a stubble beard, he turned my stream into a commercial for men's cologne.

He crossed his arms. "Do you think they'll be your witnesses? They'll help you if they have something to gain." He looked at the pillars behind him. "I suppose they would have something to gain."

"That means you have something to gain, too." I glanced behind me to ensure I didn't block the camera.

"I do," he said. In a nonchalant manner, he positioned himself so that my body shielded him from the viewers. "And something of equal value to give. I will help you find the love of your life if you help me save the love of mine. Because the love of your life doesn't exist in this space-time, right? And frankly, neither do I."

I blinked, and he was standing next to me. He reached over my shoulder and turned off the stream.

I didn't stop him. I couldn't. His presence intimidated me, as did the weapon holstered on his right hip.

I slipped out from under him when the stream ended, knocking a few items from the desk as I stumbled into the chair at the end of the table and then back to my feet.

"Now that we've prevented causality and paradoxes, I'll be straightforward, since our problems are just beginning. In seven to eight minutes, the FBI will blow your garage door open. They'll blind you with their lights, silence you with vocal commands, and demand that you surrender the machine. You'll destroy it because tech like this in military hands is world-ending. They'll place a black bag over your head and drag you away."

I panicked, glancing at the door atop the staircase, even though he claimed they'd enter through the garage. My active imagination played multiple variants of the raid, and I failed to escape every time, even in the versions where I wielded incredible powers.

"That's crazy talk. How would you know that?"

"Crazy? Me? Coming from a guy trying to find love in another *space-time*."

Valid point.

"I'm from a future spawned by a decision you're going to make," he looked at his watch, "seven minutes from now." He leaned against the desk, which hid his pistol from my view. "You turned down my request for help. The FBI came, did their thing, and you died a mysterious death. I came back to before your significant event when you were…smarter."

"Smarter?"

"Well, yeah. You're like six minutes younger than the idiot who turned me down, which makes you smarter." He shrugged as if his words were common sense. "But you're not easily convinced."

"Well, yeah. You show up in my garage, claim to know my future, and ask me to give you my spatial gateway for—"

"I don't want your gateway. I never said that." He threw a crumpled piece of paper at me.

I straightened it out to see that the written numbers matched the coordinates of my destination down to the millimeter. A value that nobody else would know. "How…" I whispered. "Did you hack my computer?"

"You, my friend, created an artificial timeline when you opened a gateway to those coordinates and freed me. Now I'm trying to free the love of my life from a similar fate. I'd love to tell you more, but we're T-minus three minutes to the end of your journey on this path of love."

"Wait, that math doesn't add up." I counted the time on my fingers.

"Fucking engineers. I'm estimating the time."

I shook my head. "But you stopped me, right? I didn't activate the gateway, so the future will change."

He laughed. "Honestly, who came up with that silly idea? Think about it. I stopped you from opening the gateway that freed me, but I'm still here. No impact there. The FBI was already on their way unless the universe suddenly told them otherwise. 'It's all good, boys. A guy from the future stopped him. Crisis averted. Nothing more to see here.' Or something like that."

He spoke to me with so much familiarity, like we'd been friends for years. His impressions, though obnoxious, were humorous and animated as he mocked the universe.

"The best you can do to change *your* future is to abandon the present. Except you can't just throw your hands into the air and call it quits. Only events grand enough to ripple through time and space usually spawn new timelines."

His explanation didn't convince me of anything. "And your traveling to the past didn't spawn a new timeline? Seems like a significant event to me. And why not change *your* future?"

"Change my future and abandon the love of my life? You won't find true love with that mindset. Or will you? The people of your time were strange creatures. They gravitated toward, and thought they could fix, those they deemed broken. Doing so made them feel better. Selfish. Never selfless." He walked toward the platform. "Anyway, my being here is just a wave flowing over a shore. I'll recede before the FBI gets here, and the shore will be as it was. But you—you're a wave that moved the shoreline." He touched one pillar again. "So I need *you*—the man capable of disrupting the flow of time all by himself. I need you to do it one more time, and you only have one minute to decide."

One minute until what? He left? The FBI? Was his timing accurate? That wasn't enough time to make a sound decision. The man continued to pull me into his rapid pace. If he hadn't shown me those numbers, I would have thought him a seasoned con man.

I repeated what he said, "The best I can do to change my future is to abandon my present. So if I leave with you, *my* future changes."

He nodded. "Yep; otherwise, the timeline will continue as-is and result in your eventual demise. In fact, you could say that I'm also saving your life. It's a two for one deal."

"Two for one?"

"I'm saving your life and helping you find love. What do you say, kid? Because time's up." The man looked up at the ceiling, or maybe beyond, as the lights went out. Sparks along the far edge of the garage door lit the room as they traveled toward the other end.

"No way!" I ran toward the platform, parallel to the fireworks along the top of the door. Various other lights waved and filtered in through the singed crevices.

The man rolled his left sleeve up and revealed a vambrace with a digital display. A few taps turned the screen red, followed by a countdown. He extended a hand for me as the timer reached zero. I lunged forward into an even brighter light that enveloped us both.

C.2 Path of Lucifer

After the bright light withdrew, I tried to stand and run, but I couldn't move. My arms and legs didn't respond. The feeling was there, similar to the morning after a hard workout.

"You sure cut that one close." I heard the man's voice above me. His boots were all I saw until he leaned over, almost upside down. "Yo."

"What…happened?"

"Welcome to the future of your garage." He lowered his arm into my view. "This thing brought us here."

"How…that thing take us…" I coughed and struggled to speak, "…to the future?"

He pulled his sleeve down and said, "Everything is a signal. Produce one strong enough, and you'll even disrupt time." He smiled and winked. Then frowned. "Unfortunately, not enough to get *its* attention."

"What's attention?"

"How about I get you off the floor before you catch a cold?" He passed my right arm over his shoulder and lifted me up. Based on his strength, he was the one who worked out. He put me down on a mattress atop a black metal frame pushed against the wall.

"I'll save you the pleasantries. My name is Nathan. And your name is Kieran," he said. "I had the idea of calling you Michael and myself Lucifer based on our perceived values, but I refuse to acknowledge God further. You know, like an ex. Why do we immortalize those who break our hearts by making them a part of our history?"

"Why am…I…only…"

"I'm a little more used to time travel than you are. Think of it as being sore after a run. I've been running for years. You just started."

I relaxed on the mattress and faced the interior of the room as he walked away. The walls lacked the scuff marks of the various balls I had bounced off them. A larger desk stood to the left, with an array of monitors stacked next to and above each other. One screen showed the news, but I couldn't see the date on the broadcast.

The stairs behind the desk looked similar, but newer and quieter, as Nathan unintentionally demonstrated when he came down. He carried two mugs in his hands, set one of them on the nightstand next to my head, and then grabbed a nearby chair. He spun it around until its back faced me and sat.

"So." He paused, slurped his drink loudly, and continued, "I need help to save the love of my life, Eve. The gateway you opened released me from a temporal prison. Our captor suspended our bodies in time; however, our minds processed reality at normal speeds." He paused again.

Nathan shifted his gaze to something I couldn't see. He had a faraway expression in his eyes and a smile on his lips, like he was reminiscing about good times. "Eve had created a temporal field that would've allowed us to live for eternity." He lowered his distant gaze and blinked several times. "She learned to control time." Nathan revealed the vambrace again. "This is another example of her genius. I think it accelerated our molecules to speeds faster than light until we reached this designated time."

I still struggled to speak. "Energy…required…to do that…"

Nathan raised his index finger. "An academic question. Since signals outside the field moved faster than the signals inside, there was energy buildup on the exterior of the temporal field. Eve converted that energy into sustainable power and used it to maintain the field, among other things."

Nathan lowered the vambrace into my field of view and opened the display. The components inside were much smaller than anything I'd seen before, but the principles seemed similar. A network of traces connected multiple integrated chips, the display, and a few other novel components.

Nathan pointed at one of three diamonds near the center of the board. "Some of that energy went into charging these power crystals, which can store up to gigawatts'—or something—worth of energy. I used all three to reach your time and come back. Unfortunately, it's now a limited resource. Without Eve's temporal field, I can't charge them fast enough for repeated time travel. I can charge them for small temporal disruptions, such as closing the distance to people." He winked at me. "Traveling through time had jarring effects on the body, as you're no doubt experiencing. Leaving the temporal field had a similar impact, so Eve made this drink to help our bodies adjust faster."

He raised the mug like he was making a toast. I narrowed my eyes, annoyed that he didn't give any to me.

"Don't look at me like that. If you agree to help me, I'll give you some. Otherwise, there's no point in wasting it since I'd return you to your time where you'd go through the same unpleasant experience."

Nathan stood and spun his chair around to remove the wall between us. "But I suppose giving you a little would help build trust. That's going to be important." He grabbed the other mug, tilted my head forward, and helped me drink the fluids.

My body responded to commands better than before, but not completely. I wiggled my fingers, lifted one knee, and breathed easier.

Nathan sat back in the chair and crossed one leg over the other. "Life was pretty good. I don't know how long we lived because time was no longer important to us. We must've watched the sunset a hundred thousand times until *it* showed up."

Nathan narrowed his eyes and stared off into space. "We'll call the humanoid entity Azrael. I couldn't tell if it was a woman or a man. Attacks came out of the darkness of its black cloak. I only saw the retraction of a bandaged fist back into the shadows after it jabbed me in the gut, and I fell to my knees. Then Azrael turned to Eve, who had physically, and mentally, surrendered. Like she knew what that thing was and why it was there. I wondered if we'd violated some law of time and this extratemporal entity came to punish us.

"Despite my attempt to shoulder the blame, or even share some of it, Eve insisted she was at fault. But I'm not sure any of our words mattered. Azrael turned and stared at me with vibrant, gold eyes. I remember feeling powerless. There was nothing I could do. The last thing I saw was Eve reaching out for me. I couldn't tell her I loved her because my body stopped moving. My brain functioned at what I perceived to be normal. I guess it took me a couple hundred years to say 'I love you' even though I thought it a billion times over."

"How do you know Azrael imprisoned Eve there, too?"

"I felt her. That's how I survived. For a century— or whatever, I felt Eve's presence, and it kept me from going insane." Nathan paused for a moment. "Do you believe there's a limit to love? Sometimes, I wondered if I was reaching my limit. Like it wasn't enough to knowing she was there, even though that should've been enough, right? I needed to talk to her, touch her, hold her, kiss her. We had transcended life, but couldn't escape life."

I moaned in pain as I sat up and enjoyed the relief after. "I haven't found the love of my life, remember? Look, I'm sorry about what happened to you two, but I don't know how I can help."

"You can help by moving the shoreline again. When Azrael came for us, this arm brace was a prototype Eve was working on. She wanted to save our time outside the field, too. After you freed me, I spent a few years learning how to use it—how to fight with it. But when I was ready, I couldn't create an event grand enough to get Azrael's attention. So I traveled back in time to ask for your help again."

I laughed uneasily and shook my head. "And if I turn you down, you'll send me back to be abducted and killed."

Nathan's silence sent chills down my spine. First the FBI, and then an otherworldly entity. Neither contributed to the fame and fortune I had imagined.

"If you wanted to find Azrael, why didn't you go back to the time where I committed the crime and confront it then? Or back to the time when it attacked you?"

Nathan closed his eyes and sighed. "And do what? I would have used almost half the arm brace's power to get there. I need Azrael to come to me, so I can fight it with the full strength of the arm brace."

His story seemed far-fetched, but *somebody* had shown up at my house in the same explosive fashion he had described. Changes to the room convinced me we weren't in my garage anymore. But the future? The components and wiring inside the vambrace could have been 3-D printed. He could have fabricated everything in the room.

I put together several more questions in my head, but a woman's voice drowned my thoughts as Nathan increased a television's volume.

An anchorwoman with light brown hair and glasses spoke with urgency. "We interrupt your local station to bring you breaking news on the group called Temporal Interdimensional Multidimensional Entity, or TIME, who had announced this morning that they would sacrifice a woman live on multiple social media platforms. The stream started thirty minutes ago with an unconscious woman tied to a large, wood-framed hourglass. Our correspondent, Jacob, has more information."

Jacob stood in front of a multistory glass building. "Thank you, Dana. Eden's authorities are working with social media platforms to bring the stream down; however, it's being broadcast from Earth, where Eden's authorities have no jurisdiction. Local authorities from Earth have stated that an investigation is underway, but finding the group will be difficult because of Earth's vast, unmapped regions. Neither government has released the name of the woman in the video."

"Wow, so this is the future?" I said with sarcasm, and then turned to Nathan and asked, "What do they mean by Earth and Eden?"

Nathan focused on the broadcast and responded in a monotone voice. "Everything on the surface is called Eden. Everything underground is called Earth. For centuries, two political parties argued over the same issues. The announcement of VoCAls divided the country in two—those who accepted the program and those who did not. The former stayed on the surface and named it Eden, while the latter were driven underground."

"VoCAls?"

Nathan pointed at the defined acronym in an announcement scrolling across the bottom of the broadcast. "Voice Control and Alteration. A division of the police that controls people using voice commands," he said.

The screen split vertically to show Dana again on one side. "Jacob, what can we expect from this group? What do their actions mean for Camille's scheduled speech this afternoon? She wants to end the Voice-Activated Collar and the Voice Control and Alteration programs. If these programs existed down on Earth, would this be happening?" Dana's brows slumped.

She wasn't asking to be informed; she was confirming something she'd already made her mind up about. I hated that kind of news.

"Those are great questions, Dana. The simple answer is no. TIME identifies as a religious sect, but they're a cult comprising individuals who have been in trouble with the law before. If those individuals had collars, authorities could track and even trigger them to neutralize those participants and end the sacrifice. If VoCAI units had authority down there, they could command the individuals to stand down without hurting anyone. And I'm glad you mentioned Camille because I'm standing in front of the Department of Immigration and Emancipation Management right now, where Camille is expected to release a statement after her talks with DIEM. Camille has been representing the collared denizens of Eden, those taking part in the Convict Adoption and Rehabilitation Program of Earth. As you mentioned previously, Dana, Camille wants to end CARPE, and instead, put a collar on VoCAIs."

"Thank you, Jacob. We'll continue to bring you live updates—"

Nathan muted the channel. He closed his eyes and released a long sigh. "I need to help that woman."

"Is she Eve?"

"No, but she's being sacrificed by a cult I created."

C.3 Path of Eden

"You started a cult?" I was hot on Nathan's heels after we left the house. Time was short, so he swore he'd explain along the way. I had several questions for him until seeing the world outside the garage derailed my train of thought.

"Where are we?" I asked. Nothing looked familiar. Not the large square pillars forming a wall on the horizon, or the reflection of the city in the cloudless sky. The usual neighborhood noises were absent. Silent cars drove down the street, and the few kids playing in a nearby yard kept their voices to a minimum.

"Welcome to Eden." Nathan spread his arms out and spun around once. "Its citizens believe it's the textbook definition of a utopia and consider Earth a dystopia."

Nathan's stride put some distance between us, especially since I stopped to investigate everything that differed from my time. There were no longer any doubts that we'd transitioned to some future.

"Yeah? What do you call it?"

Nathan stopped and turned around. He stuffed his hands into his pockets. "I don't care what it's called. Eve is my utopia. I'm not being a cheesy romantic. I'd end this world for her." He was serious, but not scary. The reservation he showed convinced me he'd make good on his words only if it was his last option.

The shift in tone reminded me of the real reason we'd emerged from the garage. "Is that why you started a cult?"

The tension in Nathan's face lessened, replaced by the guilt that reflected in his eyes. "I wanted to start a movement, not a cult. I needed to kick off an event significant enough to create an artificial time-line." Nathan started walking again. "So I found a small religious sect and convinced them I was a time lord, there to grant them life eternal. I named the group TIME—Temporal Interdimensional Multidimensional Entity."

I was jealous. Only someone with his presence could move people's hearts. Society largely ignored me. My ideas at work went unheard, my accomplishments got swept under the rug, and my social attempts further alienated me. But this guy walked into a room full of strangers and convinced them he was a god worthy of a sacrifice.

"I abused the power Eve left me." Nathan waved his left arm, the vambrace hidden beneath the long sleeve. His attire drew my attention to the style of the few people who walked the streets. Most wore light athletic gear, a few strolled in sundresses, and others sported above-knee shorts. Some squinted at me while others stared with raised brows. My generic khaki cargo pants were out of place.

I tried to smooth out the wrinkles of my pants as if my hands could work miracles or turn them into slacks. "I don't see how gaining a group of followers could create a new timeline."

"It didn't. An unnatural change on a larger scale had to occur; except I don't have decades to see one through." Nathan stopped at a large intersection. He made a fist. "Eve was my rock. For me, knowing she was nearby helped me maintain my sanity. If she ever realizes that I'm gone, then loneliness may overcome what little sanity she has left."

The intersection was devoid of traffic lights. I watched cars cross, some slower than others; but none of them stopped for each other, as if they communicated priority in advance. I wondered how well the system worked during rush hour and whether the monorails above reduced the number of people traveling by car.

The cars yielded for pedestrians. We waited a few moments before Nathan crossed the road with a brisk stride. I felt the urgency in his step as I struggled to keep up. "So why are they sacrificing a woman?"

"I told them about Eve. Sort of. The takeaway was that their devoted time would help restore her life force. And if that was successful, we could repeat the process for each member. I manipulated time to prove my power. A few heretics, if you will, thought that daily devoted time was taking too long. They were partially correct, since the intent was to get Azrael's attention, not to increase their life force. When Azrael never showed up, I abandoned the idea."

I stopped mid-stride. "So you just walked away?"

Nathan stopped, too. "I walked away. The heretics must have taken over during my absence. This sacrifice has to be their doing. I'm guessing they're trying to increase one's lifespan by stealing the remaining time from another." Nathan sighed. "Not something I taught them."

"So this is your fault. You manipulated them and then just walked away."

Nathan turned and walked back to me. "Why do you think I'm taking responsibility? And why are you trying to make me feel worse?"

I recoiled. Making him feel worse was never my intention. Or was it? Sometimes I was too hard on people. On myself.

"My number one priority was, and still is, Eve. But it won't take me long to dissolve that cult." Nathan leaned in toward me. Blue eyes focused elsewhere when he spoke to me. "In the meantime, I hope you're thinking of a way to disrupt the timeline." His eyes shifted back to me.

I nodded, even though I hadn't given it any thought.

Nathan stood straight. "We'll take Central Station's Sub-Terrestrial Elevator down to Earth. I know where to find—"

A large display on the side of a tall building across the street came to life. Nathan and I both raised our eyes to the video of a woman walking down several paved steps toward a podium at the bottom. She wore a strapless white dress that shaped her waist and gradually widened toward her shins. Natural red hair settled on her shoulders as she grasped the edges of the podium with her long, slender hands.

"Who is she?" I asked.

Several other people stopped to watch the broadcast.

"She would be Camille—an idol, a Vocalist, and lately, an activist."

"She's gorgeous," I whispered.

"I figured this place would be great for you. Most of Eden's women are beautiful. A ban on social media platforms that degraded or enhanced the visual appearance of an individual went a long way toward helping people regain their self-esteem."

I said in a sharp tone, "I'm not shallow. Beauty isn't the only thing that attracts me."

"Yeah, yeah, I figured. But it's a good start. Although, I think you'll find the love of your life in Earth. That's where I first rescued Eve. A collared rose with retractable thorns." Nathan spaced out again. He escaped with every mention of Eve's name.

"Collared?"

Camille spoke before Nathan could respond. "Good afternoon. I see that you've all gathered here today, perhaps for the wrong reasons. I want to talk about inequality, but I'm sure you want to hear about my meeting with DIEM. For centuries, these talks have always been about the impacts of equality on our society, but never about the people impacted by our society. Civil rights, women's rights, LGBTQ, and now criminal rights. Science fiction writers of legend thought equality for artificial intelligent machines was next. Surely, we'd exhausted all forms of inequality against our fellow man. That was the true fictional story."

Camille's words caused the owners of the raised microphones to lower them. Then the confidence in her voice boomed. "Why wouldn't equality for one group of people mean equality for all groups of people? Why do we keep fighting the same battles? DIEM doesn't believe we're fighting the same battle. To them, participants are serving under the CARPE program. Participants? Serving? You mean the men and women enslaved to do some master's bidding?" She raised her hand and voice, and mocked the institutions she spoke about. "Oh, there are laws in place to manage the treatment of CARPE participants. You mean the laws being circumvented by Eden's elite? For centuries, the entitled have always found loopholes in the laws, regulations, and processes that they themselves put in place. And in every instance, someone has stood up to say that enough is enough. I met with DIEM today to let them know that I'm that someone. A voice for this generation. Today, I declared war! We will see whose voice is stronger!"

Gasps rose from the crowd. The few heads on screen searched for concurrence among peers that what Camille had said was, in fact, shocking.

Camille stared down in front. "If history is going to repeat itself, then let's skip all the nonsense of protests, processes, and formalities that we know are going to take years to matter more. Let's take real action now!"

She spoke like she was starting a rebellion. Or was she starting the movement Nathan needed? Or were Camille's actions part of the current timeline's natural path? I wasn't sure. Time's complicated.

A man in the front row raised his microphone. "Camille! Are you saying that protests don't matter? That they don't work?"

Camille smiled. "Let's be honest, protests are designed to slowly dissipate peoples' rage. Stand here and chant while we go to lunch. The law says you're free to protest, but the loophole says that nobody has to listen or act. Don't misunderstand me, protests do and have worked over a significant amount of time. Time that many people don't have."

The questions continued, but my attention shifted to several gray vehicles that sped down the road, the fastest I'd seen anything move since I arrived. "What's going on?"

Nathan sighed. "That would be VoCAl on their way to silence the songstress. No doubt taking advantage of the loopholes she mentioned in order to circumvent freedom of speech."

Alarmed, I asked, "What's going to happen to her?"

Nathan scratched his stubbled chin. "Hmm, she's rallying people against the government, so probably execution, which is why we need to lay—"

"We have to help her!"

"Huh?"

I directed Nathan's attention to the reflection in the sky. I could barely make out the vehicles that drove past us, but they were the only fast-moving objects straight above. "If that's the same group that drove by, then she can't be far."

"Yeah, *if* that's the same group. There's more than one group, you know. They could be responding to another call. And if we went, what are you going to do?"

I pointed to his left arm. "You can manipulate time."

Nathan grabbed his arm and rotated it away from me. "This power only exists for Eve. And like I said before, there's limited resources to activate this thing."

I turned back to the screen. VoCAls were already on the scene. One demanded cooperation from the crowd, and everyone complied. Nobody objected, conferred with their neighbor, or gave the command much thought. Four more VoCAls walked up to the podium and demanded Camille's unconditional surrender. She did without complaint.

Nathan shook his head. "That's the power of VoCAls. If you went there now, they'd tell you to stand aside, and you'd unwillingly comply."

I was angry. My hands balled into fists and my teeth ground against each other. Just like that, the voice of reason was silenced. I wondered what kind of future I had traveled to. At the rate Eden was devolving into dystopia before my eyes, I was better off taking the love of my life back to my time.

"When you told me about Eve, you mentioned feeling powerless. Now you have power. What's your excuse?" I raised determined eyes to Nathan's expressionless face.

"Let's save one woman at a time. The sacrificial lamb, then Eve, and then Camille."

That powerlessness I spoke about settled in my stomach and warped my lips into a frown. There was nothing I could do about any of the current events.

Nathan placed a hand on my shoulder. "Don't worry about her yet. Her dad is one of Eden's elites." He looked at the pillars in the distance. "Although he's the same scum she declared war against, I'm sure he'll object to his daughter's arrest. His protest will mean more than the commoners' protest that Camille mentioned, which should buy us time."

A sad smile creased my lips. "Listen to us prioritizing people's lives. Can we really even help them?"

Nathan grinned. "With Eve by my side, I can do anything."

C.4 Path of Earth

Earth was well lit for being underground. After hearing it called a dystopia, I expected dark alleyways, overcrowding under fading lamp posts, and oppressed citizens breathing toxic air and drinking unfiltered water. Instead, Earth resembled a partly cloudy day from my time. Large, sectioned, round glass skylights spread and reflected the sun's light throughout the underground. At each one's center, a column of light focused onto solar panel farms that powered surrounding cities. From the Sub-Terrestrial Elevator that descended from Eden, the columns looked like a forest of light.

"Wow. That looks amazing," I said.

Nathan stared at the light-forest with his hands buried in his pant pockets. "It has its moments."

Varying elevation caused some areas to be geographically closer to Eden than others. The elevator we took stopped near a well-lit building with neon signs. We took a cab to a low spot at the edge of sunlight. I glanced at Nathan, nervous about the dangers of dimly lit places. The stern expression on his face calmed my nerves.

We hiked on foot until we reached a large, rundown building. We entered through two shattered stained-glass doors. "Is this a church? Seems kind of obvious for them to be here," I said as we trespassed over the shards.

"Who wants to fuck with God? Churches are exempt from several things for that reason. An abandoned one at the edge of town is the perfect hiding spot."

Nathan walked into the main sanctuary and stopped halfway between the rows of deserted pews. "Even if the police searched this place, they'd be hard-pressed to find the entrance," he said.

We left the sanctuary and entered a confessional. Nathan and I squeezed into a box made for one.

A deep voice spoke through a grated wall to our right. "Hello, my sons. What can our Lord Savior do for you today?"

"Father, I have sinned," Nathan said. "I am here for your blessing and a baptism with my brothers in time."

The back wall of our confessional slid open, startling me. I followed Nathan into a small closet. He grabbed two violet robes from the shadows and handed one to me. A fresh cotton scent filled my nostrils when I passed it over my head.

We trekked down a dark stairway with black pits to each side. Dim lights illuminated steps in front of us as the ones behind us faded. Twenty steps later, light gradually revealed the rest of the cavern. Stairways from other confessionals converged toward the round platform at the bottom. A low ceiling blocked my view of the room beyond the first row of purple blobs taking shape on the platform.

Sudden fresh air made the thick robe tolerable as the roof of the cavern opened up to the underground sky. Individuals became distinguishable as we reached the bottom. Nathan pulled the hood of his robe over his head. So did I. Then we slipped into the gathering crowd like drops of water into a basin.

Nathan stopped several rows from the front and looked up at the unconscious woman held captive inside the upper half of a wood-framed hourglass. The wind caused her wild auburn curls to brush up against her freckled cheeks. They had tied her upright with her naked arms and legs beneath a long shirt. Her natural curves resembled the structure that held her captive.

"I don't understand. How are they planning to…?" Then I noticed the skylight above. The hourglass sat directly below its center, the sun at its edge and on a path that would pass enough energy through the woman to power a city.

"Nathan—"

"Shush," he said with a hand over my mouth. "We're in the middle of two or three hundred cultists. An honest mouth like yours will get us killed."

I bit my lip and relaxed my posture. The powerless feeling returned.

I felt the crowd move. Multiple heads turned to the left, where another, more fashionably cloaked man walked several steps onto a small stage. He glided to a podium in front of the hourglass. He stood in silence for a moment and then raised an hourglass-shaped chalice into the air with both hands clasped around the upper half. I heard several whispers call him the high priest.

Gray chin hairs glistened beneath the shadow of the high priest's face. "Time. Waits. For. No one," he said and lowered the chalice onto an extruded piece of wood behind the podium. "Until now. Thanks to our Lord—the Temporal. Interdimensional. Multidimensional. Entity," he sang each word. "TIME has chosen us to take the next step toward Eden. Not the fallacy above, but the real garden where food is plentiful, man's desires abated, and time is only used to measure how long ago our sins were forgiven. Cast aside your desires! Share your wealth! And time eternal will be yours."

The high priest paused. He turned his head and I caught a brief glimpse of his worn face as he scanned the crowd with his eyes. The sound of waves crashing below added a dramatic score. "Today, I share with you my ultimate wealth." He stepped back, turned, and used a hand to direct our attention to the woman held captive. "Today, I share my favorite daughter, Aurora!"

I couldn't believe that the high priest, and a father, was sacrificing his daughter, and that the followers approved. They whispered praises of "thank you, Lord" and "your sacrifice will be appreciated." I maintained my silence and hoped Nathan had a plan as the sun's light drew near.

The high priest turned back to the podium and caressed the goblet. "The Lord's light will collect my daughter's time, and I will share it with you through this chalice. As TIME himself promised eternity through Evelyn, I will grant you, my faithful acolytes, the same through Aurora. Although my daughter is pure in many ways, social media has tainted her soul. We'll take the time she spends admiring false gods to give thanks to our lord, TIME!" The high priest raised the chalice again.

Aurora woke after loud applause followed the declaration. She looked around, dumbfounded for a moment, before she panicked. She attempted to yank her arms loose and then shook her head to clear the tears obstructing her view. Aurora looked down, straight into the high priest's cloak. "Father! Father, please!" Aurora begged, as she continued to test the quality of the knots.

The high priest turned toward her. "Hear my dear Aurora's voice, for it is the first time she has addressed me as father. Time changes people. The experience we've gained over the years. The realization of it fleeting during our darkest hours, and now, the sacrifice that will take us one step closer to Eden. We will be changed."

The sun was almost overhead. Aurora looked up, and the light caused her to squint and avert her gaze.

I said to Nathan in a loud whisper, "You can stop this if you tell them who you are!"

"Like I said, the heretic onstage has taken over. I don't know what he's said—what he's changed over the past few months. I could be the enemy for all I know. Don't worry, I'm going to save her."

Aurora called out to her father multiple times; each subsequent plea weaker until her voice faded completely. I opened my mouth to speak for her, but paused at the sight of her surrender. She closed her eyes and hummed. Her voice manifested opposite the way her pleas had—quiet at first and then louder. The cries that had been ignored as words garnered the attention of nearby cultists as tunes. Her melody reached their souls, and then it reached their hearts.

The surrounding cultists bumped me once, then twice, from behind. Had I not moved, they would've trampled over me. Everyone I saw trudged along with a distant gaze in their eyes, even Nathan. I reached out to him, but several cultists had already filled the gap between us.

Aurora's song grew louder. An overwhelming sadness accompanied it—accompanied me. I questioned my life, its purpose, and whether my efforts were worth anything. Voices from the past haunted me. Men, with misplaced confidence, looked down at me as they swept my crushes off their feet. Women smiled at me with pity while their eyes suggested I wasn't good enough for them. Yet, the music was all I could truly hear.

"No," I mouthed. My subconscious voice replaced the physical sounds. I grabbed my head with both hands. I buried those voices from long ago. Music was the dirt I used to fill their graves, ranging from successful artists to my own amateur lyrics. Sad songs had wrung emotions out of me, but never like the one she sang.

The song stopped. My sanity returned, and so did the normal sounds. I found myself at the edge of a collapsing cliff where dark waves crashed below. I saw several cultists disappear into the darkness. Many more around me prepared to follow. The ground beneath me crumbled, and I grabbed onto a wooden beam above my head. It belonged to the hourglass. The zombie-like cultists must have knocked it over, and their forward motion continued to push it farther off the edge.

I looked for Aurora. She, too, hung from the hourglass's mangled structure. Most of the ropes that had secured her came apart when the wood they tied to snapped. She made several efforts to grab the last knot around her left wrist, but failed. Each attempt weakened the remaining structure.

"Don't move!" I shouted.

Aurora looked at me wide-eyed. She glanced at the cultists as they continued to take their own lives and then back at me, bewildered.

"I'll come get you!" I glanced at the depths below and swallowed hard. I couldn't tell if rocks or spikes breached the water.

I hoped my added weight wouldn't cause the hourglass to fall over the edge. I pulled myself up and rested my chest on the beam I clung to for dear life. Then I swung my leg over the wood and hoisted my body up. I straddled the beam in the wrong direction, so I thought.

Nathan was in front of me. He meandered toward the edge at a slower rate than the others. His gritted teeth, tightened muscles, and the distress in his eyes were evidence that he fought against the lingering effects of Aurora's song.

"Nathan!" I crouched on the beam, kept my center of gravity low, and inched my way toward him. When I stood above solid ground, I dropped and ran to him. "Snap out of it, man." I stood in his way, but he pushed me back with his chest. His muscular build made him difficult to stop.

I looked up at his face as he said, "I can see her. Eve is waiting for me."

"No, we're supposed to save Eve together in some crazy fucking way, remember?" My words reached him, but he looked through me. I needed to get his full attention, so I punched him in the chest once, twice, three times, and he caught my wrist on the fourth. We stared at each other for a moment.

"Ugh, my head." He rubbed his right temple.

"I didn't hit you there."

"Even if you did, those light punches—"

"Aurora!" I turned around, but she was gone. "No way!" I fell to my knees. A visual of her falling played in my head until Nathan's hand rested on my shoulder.

"I already got her," he said and directed me toward a confused woman sitting on the ground, away from the few remaining cultists on that side of the platform.

"When did you…"

"After the third punch. Before the fourth." He observed the surrounding chaos. "Thanks. You saved me." He smiled sadly. "And her. Evelyn will be proud."

A helicopter flew behind the sun's light and circled around the cavern. It emerged on the left side of the cliff with a bright light that tried to illuminate the anarchy. "Attention! This is the Voice Control and Alteration Division. By the authority of Eden, and in cooperation with Earth, we order everyone to surrender and await further instruction!" Multiple ropes dropped from the helicopter and uniformed men rappelled toward the ground.

I covered my ears.

Nathan tugged my elbow until I lowered my hands. "It doesn't work through the microphone." He nodded at an opening to the left of the entrance we came down. "We should get going before the footmen get here. Act like a mindless human and follow me."

I nodded and then objected. "Wait, we can't leave her."

"Why not? She's the victim."

"I don't think VoCAl will see it that way." Nathan probably didn't know Aurora's song had caused the surrounding chaos. We stared at each other until the first VoCAl touched the ground on the other side of the hourglass. His vocal commands affected half of the cultists near him. They apprehended those who obeyed and tackled the rest.

Nathan raised his left sleeve. "Go get her. I'll secure our escape."

C.5 Path of Uriel

Dana's voice greeted us after we entered the garage. The anchorwoman must've been working overtime, yet her makeup remained pristine. "We're continuing to bring you live coverage from Earth. An hour ago, VoCAls took control of the scene. The death toll is now at one hundred twenty-two. Less than a hundred apprehended. Hundreds more missing."

I helped Aurora to the same bed Nathan put me on when I had arrived and lowered her to the mattress. A sigh of relief escaped her after she relaxed her bruised ankles and wrists.

I watched the broadcast. A message scrolled across the bottom: Authorities used the sunlight in the stream's background, and closed and reopened skylights until the light in the video dimmed.

A new correspondent named Kyle reported in front of the downed hourglass. "VoCAls have taken control of the scene, which is an old solar farm behind an abandoned church. The farm once provided most of the area's power, but has been nonoperational for years because of structural collapse. Some locals mentioned attending nativity plays by candlelight at the church, which really highlights some of the poor conditions of Earth."

"Do we have to watch that?" I asked Nathan.

No response. He stood inches from the monitor, scanning the wide screen footage with eager eyes.

"We were there, remember? What are they going to say that you don't already know?"

Nathan curled his fingers into a fist. "It didn't show up."

"What didn't?"

"Azrael!" Nathan punched the desk. "Should the sacrifice have been successful? No. That many deaths should have been a bigger crisis. Or would the single sacrifice have had a greater social impact?"

I stomped over to him. "Are you seriously trying to measure the value of life?"

Nathan snapped, "What does it matter?"

I stopped short, taken aback by his tone.

He turned to the screen and said, "If you're in a race and the first car crashes, do you stop to pity them, or do you take the lead and win?"

"This isn't a game. We're talking about people's lives. The people you led—"

"The people who chose to sacrifice someone else for their own selfish reasons. I led them to water, and they chose to drown others in it. If anything—" Nathan suddenly shoved me to the side.

Aurora careened past me and tackled him to the ground.

"This was your fault!" Aurora screamed, mounted Nathan, and swung her fists at his head. She wasn't an amateur fighter. She feigned punches, waited for Nathan to shift his arms in defense, and then attacked the openings. "Fuck you! Fuck… You…" As emotions overcame her, the strikes weakened. The bruises on her wrists darkened.

Nathan caught her swinging arms, avoiding the discolored areas, and said, "You stupid—get off me!"

Aurora jerked her arms free and struck Nathan with her elbow. A clean hit that exhausted the rest of her energy and ended the fight. She slumped over his chest. Both breathed heavily.

"You… You don't know anything," Nathan said under her weight.

Aurora surged up, grabbed him by the collar, and pulled him toward her. "They were going to kill me! What more do I need to know?"

Nathan grabbed her upper forearms and heaved himself closer to her face. "I didn't put you in that position!" He shoved her backward and onto the ground.

I inched my way toward Aurora, somewhat afraid to incur her wrath. "Nathan didn't mean for that to happen. And he helped me get you out of there."

Aurora whispered, "You should've let me die."

Her words almost broke me. My heart slumped in place, and a tight knot in my stomach almost doubled me over. I had never experienced those words in person before, and they weighed heavy on my conscience, even though I wasn't involved in the events that led up to them.

A photo of Aurora appeared on screen as Dana reported, "…is wanted for the murder of over two hundred people. Authorities have issued a warrant for her arrest. Anyone with knowledge of her whereabouts is urged to contact the Voice Control and Alteration Division of the police."

I'd had a hunch the police would go after her, even though she was the victim. And they'd go after her harder than any of the true criminals because she displayed incredible power. I imagined the same would've happened to me after I built the spatial gateway. My security measures hadn't been enough to hide me from the power-hungry government of my time. How was I going to hide Aurora in a future where technology was far beyond what couldn't protect me?

Aurora looked at the monitor with tears in her eyes. "My life is over." Then she yelled at the screen, "Two hundred fucking people who tried to kill me!"

For a moment, I was guilty of Nathan's thoughts. I wondered how those deaths weren't enough to gain Azrael's attention. Then it occurred to me.

I asked Nathan after he stood, "How does a significant event create a new timeline?"

Exasperated and defeated, he said, "I don't know." He threw his hands into the air. "Something that sets the world on an alternative path, I imagine."

"Okay, but how? Physically. Literally. Scientifically. How?" I knew he didn't have an answer, but asking aloud stimulated my thoughts. "For a timeline to split, there'd have to be a decision point. For example, deciding to go left or right. If that decision caused the split, that means at a very specific point in time, I went left and right at the same time. That seems impossible. How can I act on two decisions at the same time?" I paused at a new revelation. "There has to be some external agent acting as a second decision point. Only then can two paths of a decision point exist—the original and the one created by the agent." I spoke slower, piecing the puzzle together along the way. "Assuming artificial timelines are created by inserting decisions into another timeline, that means I didn't create one. From my perspective, you're from the future, which means I opened a gateway well before TIME imprisoned you, possibly before you were born. So, chronologically, at a moment when I pioneered the timeline frontier, how could I free you from a future that didn't exist?"

Nathan shrugged. "You couldn't have because I wasn't there yet?"

I was deep in thought. My spoken words were on autopilot. "The second activation of the gate, the one that freed you, must have initially led to nowhere, a non-existent prison, or an empty cell. I doubt it led to the vacuum of space, or worse things would have happened. But that means Azrael created the artificial timeline when it imprisoned you and manifested the second decision point of my timeline—your arrival at the coordinates of my spatial gate."

Nathan caught on to my train of thought. "So the real question is: how did your gate in the past connect to my cell in the future?"

"Correct. My gateway is spatial. It connects two points in space, which means… Ugh!" I scratched my head. "I'm missing something."

Nathan stared at me, the eagerness for an explanation clear in his eyes.

"The first activation of the gateway would've required both sets of pillars and two known spatial coordinates ten feet apart. The subsequent activation of the gateway wouldn't have required two sets of coordinates, and the second set would've defaulted to zero. Was zero a valid coordinate that led to your prison?" I looked up at Nathan. "Did the gate fold space on itself and create a temporal tunnel? That would mean your prison is in this garage somewhere in time."

The tension in my head had settled, but my heart pounded. I feared discovering an otherworldly truth. "It's all a hypothesis because *I* never activated the gateway once, let alone twice. A future me did."

Nathan's forehead wrinkled. "If an external decision point is the catalyst, then why didn't my return to the past create a new timeline? Why didn't our return to the future, and every action thereafter, create new timelines?"

I stroked my beard. "They likely did, but there's no real way to know."

"Then where is Azrael? Why hasn't it come?" Nathan asked.

"Because you're the only one it's after."

Color drained from his face until its hue matched his pale blue eyes. An awkward laugh escaped his lips, but he didn't accept the hypothesis. "How'd you come to that conclusion?"

I closed my eyes. "You said Azrael attacked *you*, but Eve was the one responsible for the temporal field. You said Azrael adjusted the timeline moments before I freed you, which prevented me from activating the gate a second time. Why didn't Azrael prevent me from activating it the first time? Both seem like they violated time and space, if the goal was to police those dimensions. The second activation involved you."

Nathan shrugged. "That explains nothing."

I slouched. "In both scenarios, neither of the two persons responsible for messing with the timeline was confirmed to be attacked or imprisoned by Azrael. And in your reasoning for external decision points, you realized Azrael has never appeared after *you* manipulated time. It's like someone other than you have to disrupt time, but that disruption has to revolve around you."

Nathan crossed his arms. "If Eve wasn't abducted, then where is she? She should be here—in this timeline."

I shook my head. "Azrael created a new timeline when it imprisoned you, and if that prison is at the center of time, then who knows which timeline you're from. Worse, you created a new timeline the moment you went to the future, when you returned to the past, and God only knows how many other times."

"Keep him out of this. It's all God's fault, and he hasn't done shit to fix it. Fuck!" Nathan kicked the desk over. The monitors clattered to the ground, the frames and screens cracked. Keys from the keyboard flew in various directions, as did the rest of the desk's contents.

I spoke over the noise. "With all these unknown decision points spawning new timelines, I'm probably not even the one who freed you."

Nathan choked and then growled, "How am I supposed to find Eve?"

I didn't tell him that finding *his* Eve was impossible—that he was temporally displaced an innumerable number of times across a dimension we had no way to navigate.

Nathan's temper dropped as quickly as it had escalated. "You can open a gateway to her—to the prison."

The prison *was* the best option, but I shook my head, anyway. "Not a good idea. We do not know where in the prison she is, or if she's even there."

Nathan appeared in front of me, grabbed me by the collar, and lifted me onto my toes. "She was next to me. I felt her!" he growled.

My chin rubbed against his clenched fist. "Okay, how big was your cell? How far apart were the cells? Where is the cell?"

He didn't respond.

"You want to open a gateway into a wall? Or maybe back into the temporal field that imprisoned you?" I grabbed one of Nathan's wrists and tugged until he let go. "We have to bring Azrael to us and convince it to take us to Eve."

Nathan uncurled his fists. "We're back to square one, then. How do we get Azrael's attention?"

"I can do it," Aurora said.

I had forgotten she was there, forgotten her predicament—the one that had just sent me on a long-winded tangent.

She sat with her right knee against her chest with her arms crossed over it, still clad in the long shirt and torn shorts of her captivity. We hadn't even offered her real clothes or something to drink.

Aurora looked at Nathan. "Whatever we do, it has to be centered on you, right?"

Nathan laughed. "And what do you know about me?"

Aurora frowned. "I recognize you from CARPE's website. You're one of their listed success stories. You called yourself Adam and won Eve's freedom through Karaoke."

Nathan raised a brow. "Did you recognize me before or after you tried to kill me?"

Aurora shifted her gaze. "After. I guess." She raised her other knee and wrapped her arms around both.

I knelt next to her. "What's your idea?"

She looked at me with moist hazel eyes. "I'll tell you under one condition. All this talk about time travel—future, past, other dimensions; wherever you go, promise you'll take me with you." Aurora searched my eyes for an answer I didn't have.

Nathan responded without hesitation. "Deal. But only if your idea works."

I wondered if Nathan was making a promise he couldn't keep. He did take me to a future, but I wasn't sure it was better than home. But in Aurora's case, any place that didn't want her for mass murder was better. But Nathan was running out of juice for the vambrace, and we hadn't fought Azrael yet, which meant that he was betting everything on the successful rescue of Eve.

Aurora sat in silence for a moment before she accepted Nathan's condition with a nod. "The song I was humming—the one that…you know…" she nodded toward the broadcast. "It's a remake of the song you sang to win Eve. It's on Camille's album 'Lost Without You.'"

Nathan laughed. "Well, isn't that convenient?" he said. "And useless."

Aurora continued, "My mother was purchased through CARPE. She was pregnant with me, but the buyer—the high priest—didn't know. When he found out, he raised hell. He…" Aurora paused. "He used the collar to force her to love him. Until one day, with me in her arms, she ignored his commands. Again. And again. And again, until she couldn't hold me anymore. I was too young to understand what it all meant.

"When I got older, I researched CARPE and its use of the Voice-Activated Collar. That's where I saw your story. That's also where I found Camille's rendition of your song. She had made it to remind people that those with VACs are human too—that they love and are loved. Years later, DIEM won a lawsuit that granted them the rights to the song. They had argued that anything sung at Karaoke belonged to them. Now they use the song, and your story, to defend their inhumanity. Maybe all that was convenient, too.

"No. I'd hate to think my nightmare was born out of convenience."

Aurora rubbed her bruised left wrist. "I'm a Vocalist. My voice inspires or demoralizes people. I didn't know how to control it at first. Worse, I was afraid if *that man* found out, he'd put a collar on me and use my voice to hurt others. So I spoke very little and expressed myself through photos on social media. Camille is a Vocalist, too. She moves objects with her voice. Following her account, I learned to accept my voice as a gift and control its power."

Aurora smiled at Nathan. Not the pleasant kind. The diabolical kind. "If I sing your song to Eden, I think Azrael will hear it."

Nathan paced back and forth. "I don't see how your singing will get Azrael's attention. Music is broadcast throughout the city all the time. I still think we need a significant event. Time has to be manipulated."

Aurora's fiendish grin widened. "A significant event. Yes. I will destroy Eden with my voice, and your song will be the trigger. An event that will even get God's attention."

Nathan and I responded in unison, the former quick to accept the idea.

I continued to object. "You're seriously okay with her killing millions?"

"I told you, I'd end the world for Eve."

"And what would Eve think about that? What kind of world would you bring her back to?"

Nathan gritted his teeth and shook his fist. "Can't you keep your goody two shoes off for one minute?"

I turned to Aurora. "Killing millions will create more orphans like you."

Aurora's smile grew even more menacing. "Good. Then they'll understand what my mother went through and what their stupid CARPE program does to people. Then there'll be lots of convenient stories."

I dropped my hands to my sides. "You're on your own, then. I won't be a part of mass murder."

Aurora abruptly stood. She raised her chin, her freckles glistening under the LED lights. "I don't need your help to sing a song," she said and crossed her arms.

I refused to back down. "How exactly do you plan to do that? Nathan said voice commands don't work over microphones or video. You going to organize an outdoor concert for Eden? And whatever you do, however you do it, manipulation of time has to be involved. You got that figured out, too?" Aurora and I stared at each other until Nathan intervened.

"Kieran's right," he said in a low, gloomy tone. "I would one hundred percent end the world for Eve, but I never considered what kind of world I would bring her back to. She's the type of woman who danced down the marketplace streets. Without its people, she'd hate it. There has to be another way."

After our voices quieted, the news broadcast spoke louder, and a familiar name captured my full attention.

"Camille, do you realize your words can incite fear and violence?" An interviewer dressed in a light gray suit asked. His curly blonde hair sat perfectly in place.

I smiled at the sight of Camille. She wore a charcoal gray dress that showed her slender legs down to the matching high heels. She spoke with the same conviction she had during her previous televised event. "Of course I do. I also know that they can inspire and save. Jacob, every word you and I have spoken since birth can be misinterpreted. Even, 'I love you.' I chose to use my words for the greater good, and some chose to interpret them for the greater evil."

I spaced out and heard nothing else from the broadcast, but watched Jacob's parting lips and active hands as he questioned Camille, whose responses ranged from eye rolls to laughter.

I whispered, "I have an idea."

C.6 Path of Heavens

The seven columns that comprised the wall were called Heavens, with each named after an archangel. A modern wonder, they stair-stepped toward the evening crescent moon. Not a single cloud stood in their path. And not a single thing stood in Nathan's way.

We boarded a glass elevator at the bottom of Gabriel, the second tallest column. Many of the lower floors led to retail and recreational tenants. The others belonged to home-owners and required retina scans to access. Gabriel's security system wasn't advanced enough to ignore time. Nathan identified an upper floor resident leaving a gourmet restaurant. We entered the elevator first and held the doors open like good citizens. We waited for his access to be recognized and then watched two floor indicators illuminate simultaneously. Nathan had pushed our floor's button in-between the eye's refresh rate.

The man looked puzzled.

"That's us," Nathan said. His charisma was natural, like he'd lived there for years. "The light's been finicky lately."

The man smiled and nodded. He rode the elevator to floor three hundred and sixty-three. I glimpsed into the hallway before the doors closed. The corridor was wide, and the ceiling was high. Portraits and artifacts lined the walls like a twentieth century museum.

After the doors closed, I asked, "What is this place?"

Nathan responded with a question, "You want to explain why one of Eden's idols is going to open her doors and sing this song for us?"

I pulled on the collar of the dark, ruby-colored shirt Nathan had demanded I wear. It came with black pants and designer shoes. There was no way I'd get to the top floor in cargo pants. I'd agreed and then argued that I wouldn't get there if I couldn't breathe, either.

"Camille wants to change Eden—specifically, CARPE and the accompanying VAC. She's a Vocalist with the ability to move objects with her voice, right? If we can project her voice across the city, maybe we can disrupt the collars."

Nathan smirked and nudged me with his elbow. "You sure you're not just smitten? You haven't even met her in real life. Then again, online dating was popular during your time. The Digital Age—what a time to be alive." He folded his arms and turned his head toward the east window. "Anyway, if it were that simple, I'm sure she would've done it already."

I heard him, but reflections cast over Eden by the setting sun had most of my attention.

"In fact, she's on TV all the time, singing. Didn't we establish this as a nonstarter?" Nathan added.

I turned to Nathan after the sun had set. "Based on recent events and a little research, I determined that a Vocalist's strength lies in their natural voice. It's the difference between attending a live concert and watching one on TV. The former transforms the full range of instrumental sounds, the crowd's energy, and the feelings of the artist into an experience that courses throughout the human body. And if you can emotionally touch the concert-goers," I looked at Aurora, "you can create delirium. The VACs respond to voice commands, so they're always listening. If we use your temporal vambrace to speed up the transmission of Camille's song, her voice will go farther. The compounded energy will hit the internal chips faster and overload them. Camille's ability to move objects with her voice will further exacerbate the electronic failure."

Aurora asked from the corner, arms folded, "Why do you sound like my phone's assistant?" She kept her distance in a mid-length black sun dress. Ruby-colored diamonds sparkled in the moonlight as we rode the elevator higher. She angrily tapped the glass behind her with the sole of her laceless shoe. Before we left the garage, Nathan had suggested cutting her hair to evade authorities. She had refused and threatened to expose us if we left her behind. Not that I would have.

Nathan glanced at her hair, now tied in a bun, and said, "Eve was similar. Logical. Awkward. Straightforward. Ignorant of social norms. It's the greatest strength and the biggest weakness of geniuses. Am I right?"

I shrugged. Aurora's question had hit a nerve, despite Nathan's defense. Another pretty woman mocked my mannerisms. I was ready to jump to another time.

Nathan continued, "He's searching for the love of his life, but I think he's really trying to find a place to call home. And when he does, the woman he loves will be there."

I didn't respond. Instead, I focused on the elevator doors and the three men that greeted us with guns when they opened. The elevator's emergency response turned on a rotating red light and disabled the panel.

"Put your hands over your mouths, now!"

Aurora slowly raised trembling hands to her mouth. I covered my mouth, too. Then I stepped in front of her.

"Get away from her!" One man shouted.

I wanted to tell them they were wrong, but talking had consequences. Nathan proved that. True to his personality, he chastised the men, and one fired a round into his left shoulder. The bullet passed through and ricocheted off the elevator glass. Aurora ducked. I covered her with my body and my head with my arms.

"Stop!" a female voice shouted.

Two of the men lowered their guns before they glanced over their shoulders.

"Don't fire another shot." Camille stepped out from behind the men.

"But ma'am, the girl is wanted for murder," one man said.

"*I'll* be wanted for murder if you ma'am me again." Camille glared at the man, who averted his eyes and stared at her naked feet. "They are my guests. Treat them accordingly."

Nathan slouched against the back wall. Blood stained the glass as he slid several inches down. The man who had shot him rushed in and gestured for help. A second man helped him escort Nathan out of the elevator and onto one of the lobby couches.

I stepped out of the glass box, wary of the last man, even though he had already holstered his weapon.

Aurora didn't move. She was a cornered fox, cowering in fear, but ready to pounce on anything in range. I reached a hand out to her, but she grabbed the slenderer one next to mine. Camille's.

"It's okay, love." Camille helped Aurora to her feet. She inspected her for injuries and then raised a hand to smear a drop of blood from her cheek. Camille paused when Aurora flinched and then wiped the blood away before leading her out of the elevator.

⏳

Camille sat next to Aurora on the couch opposite Nathan and me. She sat at the edge of the seat, half-turned toward Aurora. "It's nice to finally meet you, Siren."

Aurora smiled, embarrassed. "You know me?"

"I do! Well, the part you've chosen to share as Siren. What's your real name?"

Aurora's eyes came to life before she said her name.

"You've been following me for years. Did you think I wouldn't notice?" Camille sat back and crossed her legs. "I have millions of followers, and ninety-nine percent of the comments I receive are adoration for my voice, my status, and my body, despite not posting such photos. So, who could forget the girl asking about the first time I discovered my voice? Only someone experiencing the same would ask the way you did. You also favored every similar post." Camille cupped one of Aurora's hands into hers. "I felt something through those words on the screen. Thereafter, I shared your pain through your photos."

Camille searched for Aurora's evasive eyes. "I'm so sorry about your mother. I'm working hard every day to prevent—to end—to erase VACs for that very reason. For stories like yours."

"I don't mean to interrupt," Nathan said. "But we don't have much time." He leaned forward to take the pressure off his shoulder. The guards had applied a rough patch after he refused real medical attention. "I assume you alerted VoCAls?"

Camille turned to Nathan with a fierce smile. "VoCAls don't have jurisdiction up here. We're Eden's model citizens, after all."

Nathan glanced at the guards surrounding Camille's couch. "Right. They showed up on Earth. There's no reason to believe they won't broker a deal with the Heavens too."

"We have our own security. Mine were notified when you selected the floor. After I saw Aurora on the camera feed, I authorized your visit. I guess my men didn't get the message." Camille glanced at the man who shot Nathan.

"I'm sorry ma—Ms. Winterstorm. It'll never happen again."

"Sam, were VoCAls notified?" she asked.

"Someone notified VoCAls before we re-sponded. They called and instructed us to shoot her if she opened her mouth."

Aurora shuddered.

Camille's eyes narrowed. "You don't work for the justice department," she firmly stated.

"It was my mistake. I-I'll make sure they don't enter this floor," Sam said.

Nathan objected. "Don't waste your time going down. They'll just command you to give them access. Keep the elevators disabled and this floor off-limits."

The man looked baffled. He narrowed his brows like he didn't want to take orders from Nathan.

"Keep them busy long enough for Eden's doll to sing my song."

Camille's expression softened. "What is your song?"

"The one I sang to Eve. The one you stole and handed over to DIEM."

One of the other men turned toward Nathan, aggression in his movements. "Watch your mouth—"

"It's okay, Grant. We shot him," Camille said after she raised her hand.

Grant bit his tongue and stepped back.

Camille swapped her crossed legs. "What will singing this song accomplish?"

Nathan looked at me. His eyes suggested that reaching out to Camille was my idea, so I should explain the circumstances.

"Long story short, and crazy as it sounds, Nathan's trying to get the attention of an extratemporal entity supposedly holding his true love captive." I felt Nathan's glare, but it didn't faze me. I had chosen my words with care. Lies, half-truths, and misinformation would have delayed Camille's understanding. "To do that, we need to create a significant event manipulated by time. You want to end the Voice-Activated Collar program. If you sing the song, I'll manipulate the signal to carry your voice and disrupt VACs across the city."

Nathan growled. "Did you have to tell her *everything*?"

I nodded. "In all instances where Azrael showed up, the individuals manipulating time were passionate about their goals. That was the other reason I chose Camille. She's passionate about ending the VAC program. She also has the platform to reach millions."

Nathan caught on quick. "Individuals manipulating time—you don't mean?"

"Yes, you're going to have to let Camille use your vambrace."

Nathan shielded the vambrace with his other arm. "Temporal modulator, and the answer is no. This is the last thing of Eve's that I have."

"Is it more important than having Eve herself?" I looked at Nathan, who took a deep breath before he exhaled. "And remember, you can't be the one manipulating time."

Camille was silent a moment longer before she said, "Wow. Out of all the crazy comments I have read, I can't say I've heard that one before."

Nathan rolled his eyes and stood. "I told you she wouldn't get it. We're wasting time." He rotated his shoulder like he was ready to fight. "Just let Aurora do it."

"Aurora's voice can't manipulate objects, only emotions, and I'm not—" I lowered my voice and whispered to Nathan, "I'm not helping you do *that*. We agreed there had to be a better way."

"If it's the only way, that makes it the best way." Nathan's logic was sound, but that didn't make me accept his reasoning.

Camille waved a hand for attention. "If you need someone emotionally invested, then Aurora is best," she said.

I shook my head. "Aurora's voice can't—"

"I wonder how much we can accomplish if we said 'can' instead of 'can't.'" Camille winked at me. "If I use my voice in the manner you requested, it could cripple Eden. It would disrupt an unknown number of objects across the city. Hearts included, but not in the way you hoped." She turned to Aurora. "Plus, her voice is stronger."

"I-I can't—"

"Can move hearts the right way. You photographed your pain and vocalized your rage in silence. Now is the time to share your story with Eden as loud as you can." Camille placed a hand on Aurora's shoulder. "Show them what love, compassion, and humanity mean to you, and maybe you can change their minds about CARPE, about VACs—about people."

Camille amazed me. Nathan had predicted my feelings. Who wouldn't have fallen in love with her? She was out of my league, but her words convinced me I could do anything, even win her heart.

Camille said, "I believe you can use your voice to convince Eden's citizens to voluntarily release the VACs under their control."

I hadn't thought of using Aurora's voice to sway the hearts of others positively. That wouldn't have guaranteed the required result, but maybe that was my problem. I was logical where emotional responses were best.

"So, shall we put on a concert?" Camille asked with an electric smile that caused Aurora's face to light up in response. "Grant, help our injured friend. The rest of you, help—" Camille paused when she looked at me.

"Kieran," I said.

"Help Kieran set up the stage. We'll use the garden on the roof. Tell Father we're testing out the equipment prior to the ball. I'll get our songstress ready."

⌛

Camille and Aurora had walked out through the openings created by glass panel doors rotated ninety degrees off-axis. Nathan had shrugged off Grant's help, and the two remaining men escorted us to the garden.

"You gonna tell me how this thing's supposed to work?" Nathan asked.

I responded with half my attention. "We're going to put on a live show." I finished setting up the normal stage.

Nathan grimaced. "I got that part. I'm asking about *how* a Vocalist's voice is going to reach millions of people."

I opened my palm toward Nathan. "I'm going to use your temporal modulator like a carrier frequency to transmit Aurora's natural voice farther."

Nathan grabbed the modulator with his right hand. I saw sadness in his eyes. "I don't have many charged power crystals left. There won't be second chances."

I lowered my hand. "I know. To you, it's the difference between holding Eve or losing her forever. So, it's your call."

Nathan pulled a few fingers away from the modulator, paused a moment longer, and then snapped the latches loose. He slid it off his arm and handed it to me. "My world is in your hands, Kieran."

"In *our* hands," Camille said from behind.

Nathan and I turned to Camille. Beside her stood Aurora, transformed by a sky-blue dress with an image of the sun stitched at the bottom. With her auburn curls freed like fall leaves, she was an upside-down, scenic portrait of Autumn.

"Speechless. Just the way I like it," Camille snickered. She turned to Aurora, made final adjustments to the dress and a few rogue strands of hair, and then said, "Just like we talked about. Make it your own."

I made the final preparations, sleeved the modulator onto the microphone, and had Nathan help me set its parameters. "The microphone is just a focus point," I told Aurora. "You won't hear yourself through the speakers. They aren't connected."

Aurora walked up to the stand, which was set up ten feet from the edge of Gabriel to overlook Eden. She turned to us for one final vote of confidence. Camille and I raised our thumbs up. Nathan crossed his arms.

Aurora grabbed the microphone, closed her eyes, and sang.

I believe that we can shine
Brighter than all the stars in the sky
And I believe that we can make
A better world out of all this ice

Warm all the things that weigh us down
And shape the future with our eyes
Just you and me against the world
We'll make a place for you and I

A place for you
A place for I
A place for you and I
A place for you
A place for I
A place for you and I

The garden was quiet. Speechless didn't fully describe the atmosphere that serenity filled. Aurora turned to us, tears in her eyes and a massive grin on her face when the weight of her world had lifted from her shoulders.

And mine. Even though I stood behind her, the side-lobe effect of her voice soothed the uneasiness within me. Both the anxiety of summoning an extratemporal entity, and the doubt that my idea would work after having used the last charged crystal that powered the modulator.

During the performance, I had seen the tension in Nathan settle. His shoulders relaxed and his eyes gentled, not only from the nostalgia of the words but also the personalization Aurora put into them.

The ambiance didn't last long.

To the far left of Aurora's stage, a hooded figure sat on the edge of the column. One foot dangled over, and the knee of the other raised to the figure's chin. They resembled Nathan's description of Azrael, a black cloak with a hood, and a thick sash around the shoulders.

I leaned forward for a better view. However, I couldn't see under the hood. Not a single strand of hair or facial feature escaped the darkness. It was terrifying enough to set my heart racing.

I turned to Camille to see if she recognized the hooded figure, but she and everyone around her were motionless. They didn't move, blink, or breathe. They had frozen mid-clap and mid-cheer.

Nathan, Aurora, and I could move. Nathan turned to face the figure. Aurora slotted the microphone back into the stand.

Then, in a feminine voice, the figure said, "I haven't heard that song in forever."

C.7 Path of Evelyn

"Eve?" Nathan dragged his feet toward the cloaked figure. He raised trembling fingers as if he could remove the hood from where he stood.

The figure rose to its feet, its face still hidden; but strands of black hair slipped out from beneath the hood and shimmered in the moonlight.

"Eve—" Nathan stopped moving.

I stepped away from him as the figure tossed back its hood and revealed themself. A beautiful woman with straight black hair tucked beneath the sash around her neck. No makeup. No distorted expression as she looked up at Nathan's confused eyes and lowered jaw.

She searched his motionless eyes with her own light-brown pair and said, "No matter how many times I see you, I will never get used to this pain in your eyes." She placed both hands flat against his chest. "I never wanted to hurt you. Never. It was you who taught me to pick up a broken flower and plant it again. So please bear with me while I rebuild our garden. I promise this will all be over soon."

She rose on her toes and kissed him. Her puckered lips turned into a sad smile after she shifted her brown eyes toward me. The hue of her irises intensified to gold.

"We meet again, Kieran," she said.

I hesitated for a moment, afraid she'd suspend me, too. Or kill me. Her presence threatened everything.

"I don't believe we've met before," I stuttered.

"We have. Many, many times. I know everything about you."

I shook my head. "You don't know anything about me."

"I know you love her, and her, too." Eve nodded at Camille, and then at Aurora. "A hundred times I have seen it matured. I always hoped some versions of you would understand the trials and tribulations of love and why I had to take this path. I can't say that many of you have, which may or may not explain the tragic nature of your own love story."

"Why are you doing this?"

She smiled. "Nathan is the love of my life." She caressed his stilled cheek. "In this singular, mortal coil is a random point plucked from the area beneath the normal distribution of personality. But I wanted more. I wanted all of him—every point under the curve. Every deviation. The good, the bad, and the variations in-between. So I started a path that created repeated temporal versions of Nathan. His experiences trying to find me would vary each time, and over many iterations, manifest every variance of his personality." She paused before she added, "Eventually."

Her logic baffled me. Was she running a Monte Carlo simulation?

"I admit, things may have gotten a little out of hand. No one *really* knows how many points are required to fill the area under that curve. I'm using myself as a reference point, the number of temporal versions of me that have come together to create the equivalent of God's Evelyn. I am neither good nor evil. So please believe me when I say that I bear absolutely no resentment against you. And, as such, no love either. I will be Eve and he will be Adam." After she spoke, she shook her head at Aurora in warning.

I hadn't noticed Aurora move several feet away from the microphone.

"Please don't," Eve said. "Your heart will stop beating before you can open your mouth."

Aurora pressed her lips against each other and balled her hands into fists. She glanced at me and then back to Eve.

"So much for not being evil," I said.

I gave her gold irises the attention they demanded. They distracted me from contemplating why she didn't bring Aurora's time, or mine, to a standstill. Why was she still there, and what was she after?

Eve looked me dead in the eyes. "Manipulating the hearts of others is evil," she said. Then her mood lightened. "So, what will it be this time? Singing? Fighting? Crying? Admonishing? Begging? How will you try to stop me? And how will you fail?"

I understood that our meeting was predetermined based on previous encounters, which meant my actions would be predictable. I had to be creative, unless she had encountered that, too.

"Loving? Manipulating? Distracting? Negotiating?" She counted off.

I felt Aurora on edge behind me. Antsy. Neither of the women surrounding me was straightforward about what they wanted. "I don't understand. What do you want from me? What are you expecting?"

She responded with a muted smile. "I was hoping we could part on good terms." She clasped her hands together. Her subtle movements revealed a slight awkwardness. "I thought I would answer any questions you might have so that when we go our separate ways, there'll be no confusion about our paths."

"Did you freeze them like that?"

Eve nodded.

"How? Why didn't you stop time for Aurora and me, too? You could've done that and just left."

"What would you do once time resumed?" She stepped out from under Nathan.

I shrugged. "Nathan was looking for you and he's found you."

"No, Nathan was looking for Eve. That awkward dork who could dress up for the red carpet or dress down for a night of tabletop role-playing games."

"I could tell that he really, really loves you. So, why go through all this?" I continued before she could reply. "I can't find one person who loves me. You have everything and yet... Why?"

Eve pushed a rogue strand of hair behind her ear. "Define everything." The intensity in her eyes wavered. "We each brought something to the table. I was the smart one who stopped time for us. He was the charismatic one who brought joy to everyday living. Over time, he grew smarter. You can always become smarter. Our brains continued to develop, but our bodies…not our bodies." She looked down at herself and opened the cloak. She wore the same blue flight suit Nathan had worn the first time I met him, but the empty straps were black, and the rocket logo had shades of yellow and orange trailing it.

She shaped her upper body with her hands and stopped at her hips. "I couldn't learn to be sexier. I couldn't grow Cs or Ds using code. My hips wouldn't curve over time because I read books." Eve fidgeted. She seemed afraid to touch her body and her fingers mingled with each other in front of her stomach. "Nathan wouldn't have accepted plastic surgery. No, he was too kind. He loves me just the way I was—am." She paused, overcame her discomfort, and refocused her gaze on me. She brought the cloak together, and the color of her eyes ignited again. "I want to distract his eyes with my body, his mind with my intellect, and his attention with my existence."

I wasn't sure how to respond.

She calmly said, "You wouldn't understand. You're handsome, and you can learn to overcome your social disconnects. In fact, you've made leaps and bounds during your journey with him."

Eve's prior knowledge of my actions bothered me. Even if she had encountered other versions of me, I was different. I wasn't *exactly* like the others, but my logical mind couldn't convince me I knew better than she did.

"I'm no Nathan. He's an idiot who gets a smart and beautiful girl because he looks like *that*." I gestured toward him. "Even if I loved Aurora or Camille, given the choice, they'd never choose me over him. Aurora's here because of him. Camille is here because of him. Even you."

Eve released a satisfied breath. "So you do understand. This is the path I have chosen. And I apologize for taking advantage of the path you had chosen."

"I understand your frustration, but not your method. How is seeking every variation of Nathan going to make—convince you that you're sexy?"

"By viewing the world from a true neutral perspective. I will never look upon him as sexier than me and he will never think me smarter than him. We will be all of those things, but none of those things at the same time, all the time."

I frowned. "How will you know happiness if you don't know sadness?" I watched Eve's expression shift. "I'm happy because I know what makes me sad. I'm sad because I know what makes me happy. If you take either of those away—"

"I will still be happy," Eve stated. "Are you saying that Adam and Eve weren't happy? They didn't know wrong from right. Happiness is a chemical reaction that will still exist. Just like the feelings generated by sexiness, intellect, and love. We will give those reactions new meaning and history."

I shook my head. "You're not making any sense. Your ideas are all over the place. Contradictory, even."

"I see that we're not going to agree this time, either." She stepped back to Nathan's side. "I hope you'll make the right decision when time resumes. It's precious, after all. Time." Eve vanished with Nathan.

The accolades of Camille and her guards resumed for a moment before they realized something was amiss. I turned around, and Aurora smacked me in the face. Hard.

"You don't get to decide who I love," she growled.

Camille looked puzzled. She asked. "Did I miss something? Where's Nathan?"

I responded to Aurora. "I didn't—"

"You did, and that's why nobody loves you." She shoved me aside with her shoulder as she walked by. I turned around to stop her, and bright lights blinded me.

"This is the Voice Control and Alteration Division—" I grabbed Aurora's hand and pulled her back.

"Cover your ears!" I shouted at her.

We stumbled as we ran and tried to find our footing. Running straight was difficult with both hands pressed against our ears. I glanced over our shoulders. Several VoCAls chased us. I also saw Camille and her men surrender without resistance.

We were running out of ground. I knew that. The column was only so long. I looked at Aurora. Her lips were moving—shouting. I couldn't make out what she was saying, but her tears spoke volumes. She didn't want to be captured. The more she panicked, the more erratically she ran. Every time she looked behind her, the lateral distance between us grew. I closed the gap. I wanted to grab her hand, but I knew better than to uncover my ears.

I considered sacrificing myself to slow them down. They couldn't arrest me for panicking and tripping in their path. But they were five strong and trained. I would've been a speed bump.

Column Michael was getting closer, which meant we were running out of time. I saw the lights of Michael's lobby growing brighter as we approached. Aurora veered to the left after the glass doors rotated shut. We should have turned to the right. I called out to her. She couldn't hear me. I barely heard myself.

All the sounds rushed back to us when we reached the edge of Gabriel. I lowered my hands to steady and prevent myself from running off the column.

Aurora was in full panic mode. "Please don't let them take me. Please. Please. I'm so sorry I hit you. Please don't let them take me." She ran the words together. Her eyes darted back and forth between me and the unforgiving voices behind me.

"I'm not going to let them take you." I tried to calm her down. Tears soaked her cheeks, ran into her lips, and spread to me as she begged.

Fear gripped me when she stopped looking at me and peered over the edge.

"No, Aurora. Don't—" We covered our ears at the first sound of a voice that wasn't ours. Between the vertigo and the approaching VoCAls, we tried to understand each other's pleas.

"I have to. I have to," she was saying. I grabbed her elbow and tried to pull her away from the edge, but she was stronger. Far stronger than me. She lowered her center of gravity and jerked her elbow harder with each glance past me.

"Surrender, now!" I heard the command. My strength left me. I fought against the control. The voice that acted like a thought in my head. Like surrendering was my idea. A command I was giving my body.

I delayed it by telling myself not to let Aurora go. I drowned my mind with thoughts of saving her until I questioned what I was saving her from and lost control.

Aurora pulled us both over the edge.

Delta Timeline

D.1 Path of Michael

"I'm ready," I said aloud and away from the camera. Then at the lens: "Project Title: Path of Time. Current time: 0055 hours. The first run for record will trigger at 0100 hours. The objective is to open and connect two holes in space across many timelines. The system will loop through several coordinates in rapid succession. I expect many to fail, primarily due to the estimated spatial positioning of designated targets. I expect that some will miss the window and—"

"We need to trigger it now!" Aurora shouted from the other side of a square platform at the center of the garage. She ran across the back of the room, behind four eight-foot pillars, and powered off non-essential systems. The red, blue, and green LED indicators that reflected in my monitor faded along with Aurora's amber curls.

"What?" I tilted my head back and caught the blur of her denim capris.

"We're out of time! Trigger it now!"

I turned back to the computer. "Engaging in three… Two… One…"

The pillars came to life the same way I had seen them do a hundred times. White and blue sparks surged across each one. The current draw was massive, but stabilized after a few seconds. I wondered if the power grid, the electronics, and the garage could handle sequential activations. As the Michael from bravo timeline had said, the technology of the future was impressive. The light show was fascinating, even if the source could have imploded at any moment. It didn't. The system held a steady hum and whined with each new activation. Then, the vibrant energy flickered and dissipated.

"Only two?" Aurora said, after the light subsided, and the colors that reflected off the transported figures normalized. The screams had been silenced. The panic and aggression had toned down. Only the confusion remained.

"Pairs, honey. Two pairs," I said.

I looked upon the four travelers in awe, but held back full excitement from the joy of seeing familiar faces, coupled with the relief of success. If I blinked (and ignored their clothing), I could have mistaken *my* Aurora among her doppelgangers.

The pairs arrived at unique positions on the platform, and for good reason. If they occupied the same space, I imagined deformity, if not death, would have resulted. At the center, Kieran lay on top of the Aurora that had pulled him over the edge before I transported them. The Archangels, Michael and Uriel, sat to either side of them, next to a different column of the gate.

Slowly, they recognized each other. The natural attraction of the pairs first, and then the curiosity of their look-alike. Last, they surveyed the room until all eyes rested on me. Their state of mind prior to transportation adjusted faster than I expected after arrival.

"Yo." I acknowledged each of them before I wheeled my chair down a ramp at the end of the line of tables. I didn't want to sit above them, even if the rise was only a foot. "My name is Kieran, just like yours, and yours," I nodded to each, respectfully. "And the beautiful woman behind you is my wife, Aurora. Spelled like yours and yours." I wheeled my chair to the center of the room and faced the platform.

Michael glanced around. "What happened? Where's Lucifer?" he asked.

"Your Nathan has gone to a better place. However, yours," I nodded at Kieran, "didn't make it." I didn't beat around the bush because I knew that *I* wouldn't have liked that.

"Can you get off me?" Aurora barked. She moved her head from side to side with ease, but her fingers only twitched.

Kieran apologized, but he couldn't move off her. He looked up, and his temporary, distant gaze suggested he understood the paralysis. He sighed.

I said, "I'll explain everything, but first, there's a matter of individuality that we must address." I pointed one finger at the Kieran who had asked about Lucifer and the other to the Aurora of his time. "Let's call you Michael and you Uriel." I brought both fingers together toward the center. "We'll call you two

Kieran and Aurora. You can call me Williams. We'll call my wife Siren."

Uriel stood first. She didn't speak, but her long, toned legs made the statement that time travel didn't impact her like the others. She glanced at Siren and then shifted and narrowed her eyes at me before she turned her body to face me.

A few bolts slid from the cargo pockets of Michael's pants after he slid a few inches back and leaned against the pillar behind him. "I didn't exactly want to be associated with that name again, but yeah, I understand," he said with heavy breath.

At last, Kieran rolled off Aurora's sky-blue dress. He fell down beside her, onto his back, and stared at the ceiling. "Yeah, one day my body will get used to this mode of travel," he grumbled.

I wheeled my chair to the edge of the platform. "I moved you across space. The displacement across timelines caused a minor paralysis. Siren has the solution that will ease that side effect."

While Siren made the rounds dropping marble-sized, sea-green-colored balls of liquid into each person's mouth, Aurora burst out laughing and crying on the floor, an unbridled cacophony that jolted her body. Perhaps because of recent troubles thought to be left behind. Except the troubles of her timeline were one note from the music sheet, a score I had to explain despite the somber tone it would produce.

Michael spoke over Aurora. "How did you know the names Michael and Uriel?"

I took a deep breath. Despite the short rehearsal, I still didn't know how to start the conversation.

Siren made her way back to me and placed a reassuring hand on my shoulder. "What are you hesitating for? This isn't any different from having a conversation with yourself, and you talk to yourself all the time." She kissed me on the head and then looked at the group. "They can handle it."

I smiled. Who could have known that the love of my life truly existed in another space-time, and that she was more amazing than time itself? With confidence restored, I addressed the group. "I brought you all here today to talk about the common threat to eight-billion-plus lives: Evelyn Grace."

"No surprise there," Kieran said from the floor. He folded his arms and crossed one leg over the raised knee of another.

Michael looked over at Kieran. "I guess our experience has been different."

I shifted in my seat. "Your experiences have been different, but we all started from the same place. Evelyn is running a real-time Monte Carlo simulation to produce multiple variations of Nathan's personality. After which, I believe she will attempt to merge the temporal variants into one to create the perfect, true-neutral being.

"With each iteration, a version of Evelyn manifests as well. Many versions who agreed with her path merged, but there were some who disagreed." I looked at Michael. "Such as the one you encountered. We'll call the good ones Eve."

"Oh. Shit," Uriel said aloud to herself. Then to us, "So, Lucifer wasn't the bad guy?"

I rubbed the back of my neck. "It's not so black and white. First, let's call him Nathan for clarity. Second, if we plotted all the personalities that could be assigned to an individual, ranging from good to evil, we'd get the Gaussian curve—the normal distribution used to represent natural occurrence. You encountered a version of Nathan whose personality leaned toward the neutral evil half of the graph. Kieran met one hovering around neutral good."

Uriel lifted a brow, shook her head, and said, "Yeah, that made zero sense to me." She rubbed the knuckles she had bruised in her fight with Nathan.

I wheeled to the side of the platform closest to Uriel, pulled a first aid kit from the back of my chair, and offered to tend to her wounds. She hesitated at first and then extended her arm. Her hand felt exactly like Siren's. The same warmth emanated from the fingertips when they rested in my palm.

"The Nathan you met is good at heart, but he'll make decisions regardless of the impact on others. The version Kieran met will consider the impact his decisions will have on others."

Siren chimed in from the desk, "These Kierans are examples of true good. They're more about helping others the right way."

I opened the medical kit and rummaged through its contents until I found an alcohol-free wipe. I cleaned the red around Uriel's knuckles.

She winced and shuffled her feet. "And this Evelyn is trying to find the good Nathan?" she asked, probably to take her mind off the pain.

Siren responded, "Evelyn is trying to capture Nathan's personality at *every* point under the curve, like she's putting together a puzzle. Those points shift with each experience he encounters, which is influenced by her occasional tampering. When his personality molds into the puzzle piece she's looking for, she plucks him from the pile."

Kieran sat up and extended his arms back to maintain balance. He asked, "How do you know that? How do you know so much about them? Even if you're from a future beyond this one, you can't be from all our futures, or have you been moving between timelines? Based on my theory about artificial timelines, that would mean you spawned a new timeline with each move."

"And you would've had to observe us without our knowing," Michael added. "How did you know our physical locations when you transported us?"

I pulled a bandage from the kit and wrapped Uriel's hand. "Artificial timelines aren't spawned. Energy is neither created nor destroyed, remember? Only transferred. Where would the energy to spawn a new timeline come from? Instead, I believe artificial timelines are…unraveled. A temporal slice of existing energy from the original core timeline unraveled when an external force disrupted it. The time that slice took to peel also caused it to fall out of phase, which may be the reason artificial timelines don't collide with each other." I applied the last bandage around Uriel's knuckles.

"Thank you," she said.

I wheeled back, turned to the right, and pointed toward the back of the room. From the controls on my phone, I reapplied power to the massive array of monitors mounted to the back wall. As each one flickered to life, everyone's eyes lit up, except for Aurora's. She was attentive, but not impressed. She raised her knees and wrapped her arms around them.

I slid the first aid kit into a pouch behind my chair. "Unlike you two, whose second activation of the gate was powerful enough to rip a hole in the space between timelines, mine wasn't. Instead, the energy resulting from my activation showed me a glimpse of another timeline. It was like putting on a virtual reality helmet. I watched another version of me free Nathan. I didn't understand what it meant, and the energies only lasted a few minutes before they dissipated.

"I was going to activate the gate again, but the FBI showed up. When I attempted to kill the system, they shot me in the back." I looked down at my legs and hid my frown by turning the chair away from the group. I spoke louder, so that my voice carried over my shoulder. "I still destroyed everything using the panic button, and I paid the price. Or so I thought. My paralysis didn't stop the FBI from interrogating me. They wanted to know everything about the system and were willing to do anything—" I wheeled back to the ramp and stopped short. I struggled with my words and fought back the tears until Siren rescued me again. She wrapped her arms around me from behind. Her warmth filled my body with strength until I felt invincible again.

I raised my voice. "Eve saved me. She just showed up in my cell and took me to the future. Then she asked me to help save everything else." Siren pushed me up the ramp to the middle table. I picked up a diamond sitting underneath a monitor. "She gave me this power crystal. It's a man-made diamond that can store significant amounts of energy."

"That's the same crystal that powered Nathan's temporal modulator," Kieran said.

I nodded. "It's also hypersensitive to particles like no other material on earth. By spinning the power crystal at specific frequencies, I can capture the remnant particles of artificial timelines. I had generated a similar result with the second activation of the gateway, which helped me create this wall." I pointed at the array of monitors. "Above each display is a power crystal, tunable to specific frequencies, and thus, to specific timelines. Since the power crystals capture energy passing through them, we mostly saw events that transpired in this garage. We watched multiple versions of you pass through this room, including Michael's foray into the core time-line." I pointed at the center of the platform. "Nathan's cell exists right there. Eve's cell is, spatially, in the next house over."

Michael's eyes widened. "That desolate place was the core?"

"Yeah. Evelyn's simulation is destroying it. Each iteration of Nathan unravels more energy from the core dimension. And actually, the core was desolate to you because Evelyn's shenanigans caused your timeline to split from it. If you were there on a frequency different from your own, it'd be somewhat normal—teeming with people who don't know that the structural integrity of their existence could fall apart at any second."

Michael admired the screens. "This is incredible," he said. "You mentioned the gateway failed the first time. How did you build the one that pulled us here?"

"I started building a new gateway when I got here. Invested my entire savings." Siren bumped my chair with her butt. "Okay, Siren's entire savings. I came to the future with nothing, and somehow gained everything." I winked at Siren. She rolled her eyes, but they didn't distract me from her smile.

"I still couldn't get it to work properly. Siren monitored the streams like they were episodes of a popular drama series, and she told me that a version of you modified another gateway—the one that took you to the core." I recalled the hours that Siren had spent laughing, gasping, and crying on the chocolate recliner that faced the monitors. "So I looked over your shoulders using these goggles." I raised aviator goggles into the air. "Both lenses have the power crystal, which allowed me to see alternate timelines wherever I stood. You can tune the frequency from the dial on the side." I rotated the notch.

"Is it real-time?" Kieran walked over to the screens.

Aurora took slow steps behind him and then past him. She stopped inches from a monitor where another Kieran and Aurora danced across their garage. "It's real creepy," she said.

Aurora's word struck a nerve. I dropped the power crystal and the goggles onto a nearby table. "Yes, it's real-time. Call it whatever you want, but thanks to my temporal streams, I saved you from certain death." I curbed my anger mid-speech and controlled the tone in my voice.

Michael asked, "How did you build a new version of the gateway in time to pull us here? I completed it several hours ago, or something like that. I'm not doubting you. I'm just—"

"Trying to understand, I know." I nodded several times as I made my way back to the lower floor. "Fortunately, the core timeline didn't unravel all at once. Unfortunately, some of these series of events—from your arrival to the future, to Eve or Evelyn showing up—ended prior to my arrival in the future. And timelines continued to start and end as we built the wall. Many artificial timelines took similar paths, and we learned from those."

"If you could only see in this garage, how did you find us outside of it?" Kieran asked.

I paused, feeling my stomach knot from another hard question. I took a quiet, deep breath before Siren could notice. Despite her tough personality, the past few weeks likely weighed on her, too, and I didn't want to rely on her strength all the time.

With conviction, I said, "I calculated some positions from known signals, such as Uriel's voice when she sang and verified a couple of others using the temporal goggles. I derived some positions from news broadcasts on televisions playing in their respective basements, such as the story about a couple who fell to their death from the Heavens." I lowered my head. "We saw *us* die many, many times. We didn't have all the information or time we needed to save all of them, but we did our best to ensure their experiences were not in vain."

Aurora turned to Kieran and me, tears forming in her eyes. "I… I killed us," she whispered. She sank to her knees in terror and looked at her trembling hands. "I… With these hands… I didn't mean to…"

Kieran placed a hand on Aurora's shoulder. "You didn't kill anyone. We're both right here," he said.

"It was a fluke. We were just lucky." Aurora slumped in place. "I get emotional and everything around me dies." Tears streamed down her face as she probably recalled the tragedy on Earth. "Oh no, I'm getting emotional again—"

"And I'm not running. *We're* not running." Kieran sat next to her. "Nothing in the last few days has been your fault. We're all just functions of a simulation run by Evelyn. Nathan is the key variable, modified and returned." Kieran's voice trailed off after he realized the accuracy of his reference.

Aurora pursed her lips and tilted her head.

Siren chimed in from the ground, halfway underneath the lower left of the screens. She slid out with cables and crimpers in hand. "I actually found that sexy." After the others glanced at her in confusion, she said, "What? You can't be around this guy and not learn a thing or two. When he explains shit, I just grab a bottle of wine and listen. Then we have great sex."

I loved Siren. Down to earth. Straight-forward. And zero filter. I initially thought Eve brought us together, but seeing the others meant our meeting was destiny. Unlike the other pairs who had to play love's game, we had learned from their videos on demand. Our love had developed vicariously through Kieran and Aurora as we watched them match up time and time again. And when the occasional Camille stole the show, we threw popcorn at the monitors.

Uriel rolled her eyes. "Way too much information," she said.

Siren shrugged. "I don't have time to be coy. The world is ending. I've seen us miss out on genuine love so many times because of pride, anxiety, superficial ideals, miscommunication, misunderstandings, and overthinking. If you thought life was short before, watch yourself die several times."

I wheeled my chair closer to Aurora. "Yes, the world is ending, which is also why I couldn't wait for another iteration of your pairs. The skills, knowledge, and relationships you share will be pivotal. I'm certain." I took another deep breath. "We need your help to stop Evelyn, especially if she's trying to restore the timelines after separating them. The various paths we all took after the split mean the particles of our timelines are now arranged differently. Because we can't guarantee the spatial position of every single thing in any timeline, your particles may end up occupying the same space as another object in the core timeline."

Siren used both hands to crimp a connector. "That's another reason we didn't pull more of you at once. We didn't want you to occupy the same space." She inspected her work. "You're welcome."

I looked up at the screens. "We often flocked to the same locations, which increased the risk of particle misplacement had we summoned more than one iteration of you from the same destination."

Uriel grunted. "No matter where you go, shit stays the same."

I pleaded, "We can't do it alone. We don't have the intelligence, the strength, or the voice to wage this battle on our own. We need your help."

"I'll help," Kieran said. He turned to the others. "We Kierans are partially responsible. If we'd never opened that gate…"

"Evelyn would've found another way," Michael finished. "We couldn't have controlled that. Maybe her path would've been somebody else's problem then, but I'd rather not be ignorant of the world's end. I'm definitely in. Uriel?"

Uriel smirked. "I just wanna get this shit over with so you can call me by my real name."

Aurora was the last. She stared at the screens, specifically at the dancing pair, as if she wished to be in their place. She whispered, "Why should I have to risk dying so they can keep dancing?" A moment of silence passed. She rubbed her cheeks dry with her hands. Then she sighed. "I guess I'd rather not be dancing at the end of the world."

D.2 Path of Lucifer

Siren had brought chairs down for everyone and offered comfortable clothing to any who wanted them. We took turns getting changed in the bathroom upstairs. After Aurora swapped her sundress for blue jeans and a light gray blouse, we formed an arc around the platform. The array of screens was in view, but most of us stared at the slab of concrete at our center.

"So, how do we beat someone who controls time?" Uriel leaned back and rocked her foot against the edge of the platform. She sat across from Michael, with Aurora to her right and Kieran to her left.

I positioned my chair so that the desks were behind me, and sipped hot cocoa. The season didn't call for it yet, but the warm liquid healed my coarse throat. The aroma filled the air, but didn't coax the others into a cup of their own. "Evelyn doesn't control time. She manipulates time in her vicinity. She's not a god and is bound by the same laws of physics that we are.”

Kieran tugged on the navy blue long sleeve tee. It was a tight fit before it stretched as advertised. “So all that merging with other Evelyns hasn’t changed her?”

I lowered the cup into my lap. “Well, I don’t know. My educated guess would be that her brainpower has improved. If we’re merely a slice from the core, then a precise merge could rejoin particles without issue. Theoretically. But I imagine the brain, due to its constant complexity, would be more difficult to synchronize.”

Kieran adjusted his chair so that his feet rested flat on the platform. “So instead of returning particles to their original locations in the brain, their displacement could unlock more areas of the brain.”

Michael wore a pensive expression. “That’s scary.” He didn’t face the platform; instead, he turned forty-five degrees to his right, toward me. “To what accuracy can she manipulate time? Nanoseconds? Femtoseconds?”

Uriel smacked the seat of her chair several times. The orange graphic of a phoenix against her black tee was just as loud. “You nerds are getting out of control. Bring that shit back to earth. In laymen’s terms: what are you saying?”

Siren answered as she placed a bottle of wine on the ground next to her recliner. “They’re saying that Evelyn is trying to merge two lanes of traffic. And something about one car showing another some new tricks along the way.” She swirled the red contents of her glass. “Of course, if people could ever do that, then we wouldn’t have needed autonomous cars.”

Uriel raised her hand. “I want what she’s having.”

Siren grabbed the bottle and dangled it toward Uriel. "Girl, I brought down the entire bottle. Have some."

I finished the cocoa, tucked the mug into the corner of my seat, and pulled out a pad of paper. "Kieran and Aurora are the only ones here who have met Evelyn. Did you learn anything from your encounter with her? Siren and I have watched her, but not for too long. We were afraid she'd see us."

Kieran sat back, tilted his head up, and stared at the ceiling. "She seemed to know my every thought and move. She's fought us more than once before. Whatever we do, we'll have to think way outside the box."

I scribbled words here and there, drew a box, and tapped the tip of the pen at its center. "So far, I haven't seen anyone bring us together like this. I must be an outlier. One of the few who failed at opening a gateway and likely the only one to be injured by the FBI. Most of the others escaped that fate. Anyway, I think that's an advantage."

Michael leaned forward and clasped his hands together. "What about weaknesses? Did you notice any?"

Kieran interlocked his fingers behind his head. "When we met Evelyn, she stopped time for everyone nearby except Aurora and me. She warned Aurora not to open her mouth, which suggested she knew about Aurora's voice. But if she was worried about that, why didn't she just suspend Aurora too?"

Michael looked at Kieran, then through him in deep thought. "When we fought Nathan, he had a temporal and spatial modulator. We got the drop on him, negated their effects with Uriel's voice, and then deactivated them with a back door protocol I programmed into them."

"What kind of effect did Uriel's voice have on the modulators?" Kieran asked.

I smiled at the teamwork that had already developed between us. The events they spoke of were mostly outside my field of vision. I wished I could have set up power crystals in the other usual places, but there was no guarantee some wouldn't find them.

Michael straightened. "Uriel's voice manipulates particles just like the modulators, which prevented Nathan from using it during our fight. He was probably afraid of what would happen if two different sources messed with his molecules. If Evelyn feared the same, that means…"

"Evelyn has a temporal modulator." Kieran and Michael spoke in unison. Both stood after their revelation, startling Siren and Uriel.

Kieran paced onto and off the platform. "Eve had made a prototype before TIME abducted her. I guess abducted might not be accurate, but anyway, Nathan had it. He manipulated his time, but I never saw him use it on others. I guess she made another, more powerful one."

Michael added, "And if she's truly met any number of us, we should assume she has a spatial modulator, too. We also have to assume that both of her modulators are more powerful than ours." Michael sat down and rested his elbows on his knees. "Like temporal prison cell powerful. Nathan said the cell walls took days to centuries to pass through. If Evelyn created those, and we get caught in one, we're done."

I doodled across the pad as they spoke. Drawing the scene made the ideas clearer. "If Evelyn is constructing the temporal field using technology similar to the temporal modulator, does that mean we can get through it with one of our own modulators?"

Michael snapped his fingers. "Not through, but theoretically, we could move from one spatial position to another and bypass the temporal field. We broke my spatial modulator, but I can build another one. It'll take time."

I grinned. "I have all the required components."

"Sweet!" Michael returned the smile. "Now, with a temporal modulator, we might be able to speed up the particles slowed by Evelyn's field. I don't know enough about the temporal modulator, to be sure. I don't think we have one. And I don't know how to make one."

Kieran patted his pockets like he'd forgotten his wallet. "The temporal modulator. Aurora—" Kieran smacked his forehead with the palm of his hand. "Shit, we left the temporal modulator on Gabriel."

"No worries," I said and dropped the pad in my lap. "We can learn to build one. Our three minds will be better than the one. We'll still need to bring Evelyn's guard down. With her improved brainpower and both modulators, we can't exactly run straight at her."

"Evelyn's weakness is her mind," Aurora said. She had been watching the screens the entire time, cross-legged and with her back to us. "On Gabriel, when she spoke to us, she seemed unstable. That's what I wanted to tell you then; when I couldn't speak. I know a crazy bitch when I see one."

Kieran sat down, nodding his head. "Evelyn's words and goals were all over the place. She claimed she didn't love or hate anything, but talked about loving each other with everything, and at the same time, redefining love."

Siren refilled her glass. "Either she's crazy, or her merged desires are in conflict. Or both."

I hadn't thought about the instability of merged minds. If Evelyn had already reached true neutral, all the pieces of her minds would've coexisted in harmony. But what if she wasn't there yet? I had thought about the result, and whether it was achievable, but not about the path to get there.

Aurora turned around with focused brown eyes. "I can make her instability worse."

Michael slouched forward like the days wore on him. "That might prevent Evelyn from using the modulators. Except, she's likely seen that tactic, since we used Uriel's voice against Nathan."

"Then use Nathan's voice against her." Aurora turned back to the screens. She moved her head from one end of the array to the other, like she was looking for a specific scene. I couldn't tell which couple she watched. The way one pair moved their arms and distorted their faces suggested they were arguing. Another pair sat at the desk and munched on snacks while they worked on their respective computers.

Uriel raised her empty glass. "Great idea! Nathan knows everything about her. It was always Eve this and Eve that. He never shut up about her. Lover boy loved his girl."

Siren said, "And he comes with a temporal modulator. It's how he always returned to the future after you freed him in the past."

Michael walked up to me. "Williams, you never opened a gateway, which means the Nathan of this timeline is still in his cell, right?"

"But if we free him, we might get Evelyn's attention sooner than we want," Kieran said.

I turned my chair around and headed up the ramp to my computer. "Yes, Evelyn shows up after we free Nathan and then manipulates aspects of the timeline to help his personality deviate. However, I believe Evelyn is in control of this experiment and will only show up when *she* placed Nathan in a position to be freed. That moment, for this timeline, may have passed."

Michael slid his hands into his pockets and looked at me. He seemed unsure about something. "How did your timeline unravel from the core if you never freed Nathan? Or did that happen when Eve showed up?"

I rotated my chair and posted against the desk. "Eve forced us out of the core timeline to hide us from Evelyn. I don't know for sure, but I think she, and Evelyn, can slip into timelines without disrupting them. I suspect that her timing would have to be perfect."

Kieran walked up and placed one foot on the rise the desks sat on. "Let's do it."

I looked at him and then glanced at the others. "Are we sure? We might unravel this timeline, too."

After nobody objected, I said, "Clear the platform." Everyone backed away from the center. I entered the coordinates for Nathan's cell—the coordinates for the right side of the platform where two of the four pillars stood. "Engaging in three, two, one…"

The pillars powered up and wailed. Their activation lasted a second before sparks and spatial distortions dispersed. Nathan stood between the poles in the same flight suit I'd seen a hundred times before.

Seeing him on the screens didn't compare to his actual presence. Confidence radiated from him even after he stepped forward and fell to one knee. I ensured the system powered down completely before I nodded at Siren. She walked onto the platform to help Nathan acclimate.

"Hey, it's okay," she said. She placed an arm on his back and waved the other out in front of him.

Nathan tracked the waving hand until he saw Siren. Then reality woke him. "Eve! Where's Eve?" He knocked Siren over when he stood.

Kieran and Uriel ran to Siren's aid. I commanded my legs to do the same and then gritted my teeth behind clasped lips.

"I'm sorry… I'm so sorry," Nathan said to Siren and briefly to us with quick glances. "Where am I?"

We explained everything. Nathan absorbed the tale of our timelines well and understood the severity of the combined events.

"Oh Eve, what have you done?" he said in a dull tone.

I wheeled down to the platform's edge. "We thought you might know something that could help us stop her."

"Save her," Kieran said. "We want to save her. I promised the Nathan of my time that I'd help rescue Eve."

I nodded and acknowledged that I needed to choose better words next time.

The overall mood of the group dropped from their heightened state of alert, which reassured me that Kieran was the best one to lead the group when the time came.

Siren brought the last of the dining room chairs down and placed it between Michael and me. Nathan sat with his chest against the chair. He roughly ran his fingers through his black locks, tightly grabbed them halfway, and coursed his fingers out the back. "I loved Eve before her life was turned upside down. And I became her world after she lost everything. She dedicated every day of her life to saving me as one would save the world, I suppose. Despite both of us being full of life, she wanted to prevent the eventual end. I supported everything she did, even though most of it was well over my head. No matter what she tinkered with, I stood beside her." Nathan stared at his hands. "I never imagined that this would be the result—that my tinkerer was messing with time on a scale that could end all life." Nathan looked up at us. His eyes darted back and forth between us. "She doesn't mean to. Ending life was never her goal."

Michael crossed his arms. "It was yours, once."

Nathan's distant gaze suggested he recalled the referenced part of Michael's story. His confidence returned, and he glared at Michael. "I'm not responsible for what another version of me did. I'm also not responsible for the path Eve chose." Nathan stood, knocking his chair over, and startling everyone else. He walked to the array of monitors. "Your mathematical curve says it all. Everyone has the potential for good as much as evil. Regardless of which surfaces, all of our actions have consequences. Eve's consequences are out of this world. Mine are taking root, and I'm certain that yours are being watered." Nathan turned around to face us. "I may not have Eve's intellectual gifts, but I learned from her; the greatest mind in existence."

Kieran crossed the platform and faced the taller Nathan. He was a few inches shorter, but stood eye to eye like they were on even ground. "Like I said, we're trying to help Eve. Our challenges may not have been as great as hers, but we've all been through some crazy shit lately. We need your help, man."

Nathan closed his eyes. "Eve has no weaknesses. She is, for all intents and purposes, perfect. Even if she did, I wouldn't tell you. I could never betray the love of my life even if she threatened—well, I guess she is threatening the life of every living soul." Nathan opened his eyes and looked at Kieran. "But I want to help her. Maybe you'll find some answers from the path that led us here—the Path of Grace. I was a politician's son when I met her…"

D.3 Path of Eden

"Don't look so down, Nathanial. People will think you're unnurtured. Your demeanor is a reflection upon me and the office I hold," my dad said after he poured himself a glass of whiskey from the SUV's supply. He never sat next to me; always across from me, so he could gauge whether I was a success or a failure. I had the pleasure of looking at his hard jawline, softened by gray hairs and age.

I rolled my eyes. "Ah yes, the office of Gregory Valentine. Resident of Uriel. Out parading a nice boat in a shitty pond."

Dad leaned forward and narrowed his eyes. "You gonna test these waters today, boy? I'll drag you to the bottom of the lake." He glared at me for a moment with his steel blue irises. "I don't like that mouth of yours, but it, and your looks, are the only things worthy of being my successor." He sat back and crossed one leg over the other. "We just need to tame that mouth a bit." He swirled the whiskey in its glass. "It needs more tact. Your words should sabotage your opponent and inspire his people at the same time."

I crossed my arms and looked out the window. The streets were empty, cleared of all pedestrians and vehicles within a quarter mile of us. "And what if my opponent is the people? As it so often turns out to be."

Dad downed the whiskey and slammed the empty glass into the cup holder. "You make them disappear."

I watched his snarl morph into a smile as he exited the vehicle. I put on a similar expression and fastened my black suit jacket, which looked the same as his. Scott, Dad's public relations representative, stepped out of the passenger side of the vehicle in front of us. He fastened his jacket, too, and then stroked his blond hair back behind his ear.

A man in a white lab coat over what looked like a blue flight suit greeted us at the bottom of the stairs. He flashed a full-colored patch above his left breast when he adjusted the coat. Two others, without coats, accompanied him. Both appeared calm and focused. They wore blue flight suits, too, with more straps and pockets than slotted gizmos. The same earth-shaped patch, with a rocket ship blasting out from behind the planet, sat above their left breasts. Some of the segments of their logos varied between grayscale and full color.

Scott shook their hands. "Good morning, Dr. Serial. Thank you for having us," he said, and then denied them a chance to shake our hands with a casual gesture toward the facility.

Dr. Serial adjusted his white coat again and pulled it farther over his full-colored patch. "The pleasure is really all mine. Thank you for taking the time to visit. I know you're very busy." After a long, awkward silence, he announced with enthusiasm, "Welcome to the Institute for TIME. We are rocketing the world forward using technology, information, mathematics, and engineering. Please, come inside."

We trekked up several sets of stairs, each with ten to fifteen steps. At the top, two large glass doors slid open. The scent of chilled metal greeted us. We entered a lobby lavished by light through glass pane walls and a sun dome. A full-color mosaic matching the patch Dr. Serial and his men wore dressed the lobby entrance floor. The institute's title formed a ring around the mosaic, which rotated beneath a glass layer that protected pedestrians from its slow motion.

I tuned out most of the doctor's rambling as he paraded us to the point of interest, where two men armed with batons and flashlights stood outside a pair of frosted glass doors. They swiped their cards at the same time and opened their respective doors. We left the corridor's black aluminum tiles and stepped onto pale blue ones that reflected shades of silver from the counters that encircled the room.

Five people occupied the room. Two men stood like blue drapes in the back. They wore colorless patches like the security men outside the door. A woman in a white coat with a clipboard pressed against her chest stood next to a security guard holding a shackled man in place. The shackled man wore an orange jumpsuit and a dispassionate look in his eyes.

Dr. Serial stood on the other side of the security guard. "Sir, let me introduce you to our lead researcher." He motioned to the woman standing next to him and then whispered to her, "Introduce yourself."

She stuttered and fumbled with the clipboard in her hands. She glanced several times at Dr. Serial as if her presenting was not what they had discussed.

He urged her forward again.

She clutched the clipboard tightly and pushed a couple of strands of black hair back behind her shoulder. With confidence, and a voice that won my heart at first sound, she said, "Good morning. I'm… My name is Dr. Evelyn Grace. I am the lead researcher for the Voice-Activated Collar."

Eve grabbed a large, metallic neck brace off of an adjacent counter. She rotated it until its orientation matched the one around the neck of the shackled man. "Each collar features vital sign monitoring, three-dimensional video and audio recording, millimeter accuracy for positioning, and programmable voice recognition and commands."

Dad asked, "So if I tell him to do something, he'll do it?" Dad adjusted his posture, but never took his eyes off the shackled man, who stared back in defiance.

Eve's head flinched back. "Um, this isn't like voice control and alteration. If he moves after receiving that command, the accountable party will be notified. While the Voice-Activated Collar can understand almost any command, the responses are limited to notification, followed by an update to the sentence if applicable. I believe this encourages participants to—"

"So, no penalty," Dad said. He glanced at Scott and then at Dr. Serial before he faced the shackled man again.

Dr. Serial stepped forward. "We designed the VAC," he paused to make sure we understood what the acronym meant, "to facilitate the return of convicts to society."

Dad raised his chin and looked down at the shackled man, whose eyes rebelled. "Dr. Serial, I'm well-versed on the agenda of my campaign. However, I cannot facilitate the return of convicts to society without a means of controlling them. I must assure the peoples' safety. I need an immediate resolution for insubordination."

Dr. Serial opened his mouth but didn't speak at first. Then he said, "I don't understand what we could—"

"The accountable party needs a means to incapacitate the convict." Dad took one step closer to the shackled man, who attempted to sit upright before the guard stopped him. "Because if a man like this raises his hand to my throat, he'll kill me before I'm notified, and an update to his sentence will be negligible."

Eve stood next to the shackled man. "Sir, with all due respect, that would be inhumane of the accountable party—of the institution to implement. The system can measure the completion of a command, but it cannot determine whether the action is ethical. Participants would lose the ability to turn down unethical commands without being punished."

Dad crossed his arms behind his back and turned toward Eve, startling her. Before he could impart his wise words, Dr. Serial intervened.

"That's an excellent insight, Dr. Grace. I will go over the statement of work with Mr. Valentine and address your concerns. In the meantime, why don't you show Mr. Valentine's son around the facility?"

Color drained from Eve's face. She looked at Dr. Serial in disbelief. The drapes behind her moved. They congratulated her on the presentation as they ushered her toward the exit.

I followed. As we headed to the door, I overheard Dr. Serial's sloppy apology to Dad, who replied, "I think it's important for your leads to better understand relationships. Words like inhumane and unethical are incendiary to my campaign…and *our* relationship."

Outside, Eve stormed down the corridor. I waved the institute's men off and took several long strides to catch up to her. "Dr. Grace," I called out several times. Her long, black ponytail braid swayed, emphasizing the speed of her walk. "Eve!" At last, she heard me.

She came to an abrupt stop and turned around. "Oh, I'm so sorry," she said. "I just…a lot on my mind…" She fidgeted with the lanyard around her neck and avoided eye contact, but her full-colored patch caught my attention.

"I noticed," I said.

She didn't respond.

I side-stepped into her field of view but remained several feet away. "You don't have to hold back or be formal around me. Like you, I'm just kinda along for the ride."

"I'm not just along for the ride." Eve retorted.

"You're right," I said with hands up in defense. "We're not going anywhere without you, so you're definitely in the car. Dad's driving. Dr. Serial is in the front passenger seat doing whatever. You and I are in the back, navigating."

"Are you calling me a backseat driver?"

"Backseat…engineer. You know, instead of driver."

Eve raised her eyes to me and offered a genuine smile. "Now you're just making fun of me."

I maintained my composure despite the butterflies in my stomach. "My mouth gets me in trouble all the time. It was ready to assert itself like a ventriloquist in there."

Eve laughed. Subtle at first and then suppressed.

"My dad can be an ass sometimes. All the time, really. It's his defense mechanism when shit goes over his head. And I'm pretty sure everything you said went well over his head."

Her contained laugh spilled. It pushed her cheeks up, returned color to her pale skin, and energized her eyes. "And you understood what I said?"

I stuttered. "Oh. Yeah, absolutely."

She pushed the clipboard up against her chest with both hands and waited for me to elaborate.

"Um…yeah. Basically." I looked at her large brown eyes, one with its brow raised. "For example, if you commanded me to come with you, I'd drop everything and go."

Eve blushed. Her cheeks matched the exit sign above her head. When I thought she would dash through the door below it, she said, "Mr. Valentine, I asked you to explain what you understood from my earlier presentation. Your insubordination would have incapacitated you, as your father requested."

She spoke in the manner Dad expected of me. Words that slit my chest open, but gave hope to the people rooting for my failure. All in an accent befitting a wealthy heiress.

She dropped the act. "Anyway, you'd have to be a convict to get a collar." Eve's brows furrowed.

"What would others say about your crime other than your corny pickup-line is worthy of a life sentence?"

One part of me stood dumbfounded. Nobody ever asked me that before. Another part of me was quick to respond, because Dad said hesitation was a weakness. "My crime would be falling in love. I'm a romantic."

Eve rolled her eyes. "Make that two life sentences. I should show you around before you leave empty-handed. I'm sure your father expects you to spend time planning world hunger, not flirting." Eve swiped a card at the nearest door. A light above the reader flashed several colors before it steadied green. Eve planted her feet and forced the large black door open.

I shouted after her, "And what if I solved world hunger?" I hesitated, then slipped into the room before the door shut. A hiss escaped the hinges. I strolled into the expansive room. Monitors and keyboards lined the countertops. Scattered components, wires, and things I knew nothing about occupied the spaces between work stations.

Eve walked toward the room's center. "This is one of our development rooms. Once our researchers come up with an idea, they build initial prototypes—"

"What if I ended world hunger?" I asked again.

Eve leaned over a cylindrical glass container and motioned me over with one finger. "This is one of my designs," she said. I watched a small metal ball elevate to the center of the case and hover in place. Eve stroked the keys of a nearby console without looking. A field emanated from the ball and blurred my view of it. A muffled hum resounded from within. Eve lifted the case, careful not to avoid striking the field with the glass. She picked up and flicked a coin toward one side of the field. When it reached the outer edge, it rotated in slow motion until it exited the other side, where it regained its initial velocity.

"How did you do that?"

"Magnetic fields. When I attract the coin, I increase its velocity. When I repel the coin, I decrease its velocity. You could also say that I'm manipulating time because I can control when the coin reaches its destination."

"So, you want to control time?" I moved closer to the device as an excuse to stand next to Eve. She was a living and breathing magnet.

"I want to slow the spread and progression of diseases, viruses, and other foreign objects in the body and increase the time someone has to fight—to live. This design is too large, and acceleration and deceleration of particles using energy would be better. I also need precise control; otherwise, I'd slow or speed up other organs by accident." Eve flicked another coin into the field and smiled as it moved through.

I rested my wrists on the counter and looked at Eve through the field. "Is it possible to stop an object completely?"

Both of us raised our heads above the field. Eve's eyes lit up. "Theoretically, sure, but you have to be careful." She tapped on the console keys. The coin stopped moving near the edge of the field. "Moving particles generate heat. Slowing those particles down will make them cold and potentially freeze them. So you have to generate the energy required to counter only the object's movement, which is manipulation at the cellular level and perhaps not the molecular level." Eve looked back at the device.

"If you speed up particles enough, can you reach light speed?"

Eve laughed.

I searched my memory for the right term. "Faster than light? I don't know what it's called."

"What do you know about light speed?" She tried to cover her laugh with a hand.

"I'm going to promote the first light speed engine." I leaned against the countertop and stared at a blank wall beneath the cabinets. "That'll be my legacy, according to Dad."

I watched Eve's smile from the corner of my eyes because if I looked at her, she might've stopped.

She said, "Yes, light speed is acceleration of particles to the speed of light. If you go faster than light, I believe you'd break the temporal barrier and traverse time."

I raised my head and hit the cabinets above. "Like…to the future?"

Eve laughed and patted me on the head. "Aw, do you need a band-aid?"

I swatted her hand away and rubbed my head. Then I mentally kicked myself in regret. Being touched by her felt nice, and I'd ruined the moment.

Eve rested on her elbow on the countertop. "You don't want to go to the future," she said. "If you go beyond the timeline frontier, you'll cease to exist. If you stop and occupy the same space as another object, well, conjoining molecules will be an unpleasant interaction." Eve stared at me while I pondered her words. "Why do you want to go to the future?"

I mimicked her posture with my left elbow. "I want to see if I made you happy."

Eve bit her lip, released it, and said, "Both require a significant amount of energy…"

I walked closer to her.

"The technology doesn't exist yet…." she added, as I passed an arm around her lower back.

She stopped me at the elbow. "Mr. Valentine—"

"Call me Nathan."

"Mr. Valentine," she repeated, but slower this time. She slipped out of my reach. "I appreciate your interest. It's flattering that you'd end world hunger for a date with me. Maybe a bit too much." She brought her index finger and thumb close together. "You seem like a great guy with ambition, goals, and the drive and resources to reach those. We're similar in that respect, but we're from two different worlds."

I picked up the coin and flicked it into the field. "Last I checked, we're both on the same planet."

Eve laughed. "Oh? Is a resident of the Heavens acknowledging Eden? Earth, too? Anyway, you know what I mean." She stared into my eyes, as if to ensure her next words would reach me. "You'd solve world hunger for a date. I'm trying to help people because it's the right thing to do. These are two different paths that don't cross."

I didn't back down; I couldn't. Every time she laughed, I fell in love. Every rejection felt like a subtle hint at a better path and inspired me. I placed my right hand in my pocket. "Then help me."

Eve blinked several times. No witty response. She was speechless. At last, I'd stumped *her*.

"Take me under your wing. Show me the path you're talking about. We'll bring our ideas to life and save the world together. That'll be where our paths cross."

Eve blushed. She lowered her chin and averted her gaze. She smiled, and I felt her energy rise. "Then let's start over on the same path." She turned around and extended a hand. "Hi Nathan, I'm Eve."

⧖

Two weeks later, I started my assignment at TIME fully clothed in their sacred attire. White coats belonged to those with doctoral degrees. Various color levels of patches differentiated the rest of us. The outer ring spelled TIME and represented the engineering department. The planet referenced the information department, the rocket belonged to the technology department, and the mathematics department colored the rocket's flames. I didn't qualify for a coat and had managed a light gray visitor patch.

I swiped my badge at the entrance. The authentication failed. A man at the security desk checked my credentials and shook his head. "I'm sorry, sir, you're not in the system."

I smiled half-heartedly. "Clearly, I have a badge." I wiggled the plastic in my hand. "I spent the last two weeks going through your security process. Check it again. I'm Nathanial Valentine."

"I'm sorry, sir, but I still don't see you in the system. You will need an escort, but I don't see—who is your sponsor?"

"Dr. Evelyn Grace."

The man tapped at the keys for several minutes before he shook his head again. "There's nobody here by that name. Are you sure—" He glanced up at me—at my stern expression and then back down. "Let me check something." He whittled away at the keys some more before he said, "I'm sorry, sir, Dr. Grace is no longer with the institute."

"What? That's impossible. There has to be a mistake. She was just here—I was just here a couple of weeks ago!"

"I'm sorry, sir. I don't know. Without a sponsor, I can't grant you—"

I bolted to the elevators. Fear crippled me. My stomach knotted. My vision blurred.

"Mr. Valentine!"

I repeatedly tapped the aluminum space that surrounded the elevator button until the intended target illuminated.

"Mr. Valentine!"

After the doors opened, I rushed into the empty compartment and selected Eve's floor. The button didn't turn green. I swiped my card several times.

"Mr. Valentine!"

I raked my fingers across all the keys, smacked them with my palm, and then punched the panel before the institute's security guards grabbed me. Three of them wrestled me out of the elevator and into the lobby. They threatened to throw me out onto the steps until someone stopped them.

"Wait! Let him go!" Ed, a middle-aged man and head of security, ran out of an office to the far left of the entrance.

I adjusted my clothing, as did the security guards.

"Mr. Valentine, I'm sorry to inform you that Dr. Evelyn Grace passed away last week. There was an accident in her lab. We couldn't find next of kin. If you know any…"

The rest of his words faded. Eve's face flashed before my eyes, her voice resounded in my ears, and her laugh tore through my broken heart. I stumbled toward the exit and swung my arm wildly at the security guard, who reached for the door in front of me.

Ed asked me to return the uniform, but I refused to give them my only physical memory of Eve.

D.4 Path of Earth

Two years after Eve's death, I received an anonymous mobile message that read: *Karaoke 0018 9:00 PM.*

I asked the sender to identify themselves. The app showed a reply was in process. Several minutes later, my device received the message: *Making amends.* A digital ticket for Karaoke followed.

I sent multiple messages into the digital void. When I tried to call, an automated operator informed me I could not contact an anonymous user. My personal security determined that the phone number belonged to TIME. I requested secrecy at the highest level and to destroy all traces of the investigation.

I stared at the digital ticket. Karaoke was a program developed by DIEM to give Earth's citizens a chance to take part in CARPE. Gone were the days of winning appliances, cars, and vacations. People were the prize. And my dad's successful promotion of the Voice-Activated Collar had made the acquisition of convicts possible.

Heavens' residents paid handsomely for the thrill of having tamed felons in their homes. Prison bullies became bouncers. Gritty men and women doubled as arm candy to red-carpet events and galas. And the occasional drug trafficker wore a three-piece suit and opened car doors. Very few people adopted convicts found guilty of heinous crimes.

I took Gabriel's elevator down to Eden. The ride time was like Uriel's since our home was equivalent in altitude, one column over. After his "promotion" to Gabriel, dad had turned his attention to column Michael and started planning his next big reveal, and it wasn't the light speed engine.

I ducked my head and stepped into the back of a black SUV. A collared citizen avoided eye contact with me as he held the door ajar. He turned around, away from the door, and sat in the front passenger seat after the driver asked for my destination.

"Karaoke. Designation 0018."

The collared driver entered each letter into the system. I had never paid so much attention to the navigation display before. I was anxious. My heart raced as I wondered what awaited me at Karaoke from TIME. Maybe the person responsible for Eve's death wanted amnesty. I still couldn't believe that Eve had made a mistake. The coroner had determined that her death was an accident, but the institute provided little information, citing legal reasons.

"Sir, that destination is in Earth."

I nodded.

"Affirmative. I'll contact Earth—"

"Don't." In my peripheral, I saw the driver's eyes in the rear-view mirror. "I'd like to keep this trip off the books. Drop me off at the nearest elevator."

"Yes, sir." Gone were the days of questioning my decisions and warning me of the consequences of my actions. The collar dissuaded that behavior, too.

⧗

Earth had developed quickly. The last time I had ventured into the underground, lamp posts illuminated the streets during the day. The recent completion of sun domes provided natural sunlight and also solar power. Earth's independence from Eden was being realized.

The elevator reached Earth. I walked two miles to the destination marked on my phone. I kept my hands in my pockets and pretended to drown the chaotic noises of car horns, advertisement, and banter with headphones. A hood shielded most of my face from view, though I doubted anyone would recognize me. Unlike dad, I avoided the spotlight.

Grills along the sidewalks sizzled. Sliced fruits lacked the lush colors of manufactured goods. The scents tempted me, but the knot in my stomach wouldn't have supported eating anything. Everything in Eden was artificial—designed to smell, taste, and feel good. They could never emulate the fresh ingredients used in Earth.

Eden also lacked an attraction as vibrant, colorful, and energetic as Karaoke Designation 0018. The muted colors of the holy land didn't compare to the neon hues of this place.

I kept my head down and shuffled inside with a few others. Young to middle-aged people packed the place. I walked between them, often sideways, to avoid knocking anyone over with my shoulders. Trance music blared over the loudspeakers.

I scanned the flashy room titles above each entrance for the one that matched the ticket: Main Event. At six feet tall, I had an advantage. I peered over most heads and stood on my toes to scout a path. When I reached the designated room, a woman accosted me.

"Hey buddy, line starts back there." She smacked vibrant yellow gum and nearly swallowed it whole to put on a smile after we made eye contact. "But you can cut in front of me, handsome."

"He better get his tall, skinny ass to the back." A man, two spots behind her, snapped his fingers in the air and pointed toward the back.

The main event line started near the building's entrance. I sighed at the thought of standing in line. Worse was knowing how close to the answer I stood. The show started in five minutes at 9 pm.

My phone vibrated. A message from Karaoke read: *Participant requested at Main Event.*

I stood like a well-chiseled column. People flowed around me as I stared at the phone and wondered if the message meant I could skip the line. I didn't want to draw unnecessary attention, especially from those who had already objected when I stood near it.

Another message flashed across the screen: *Last call. Participant requested at Main Event.*

I shook my head, stuffed the phone back into my hoody's pocket and walked to the front of the line. The few who had objected before cried out again and got the attention of a nearby bouncer.

"The line's back there," the bouncer said in a brisk tone.

I raised the phone. "This thing keeps telling me to come here."

The bouncer squinted at the screen and then sighed. He scanned a barcode on the ticket. "You're late." He nodded toward the entrance. I ignored the additional protests and transitioned from a loud cacophonous room to one silenced by the voice of a single performer.

A woman serenaded the crowd with a discordant wail. Her voice engrossed the audience, so I dismissed the lack of talent as a generational difference and preference in music. I focused on the instructions that pinged my phone, looking up sometimes to avoid collisions.

"You're late." A woman, dressed louder than her clap to get my attention, stepped out in front of me. The embedded stones in her vest and pants reflected colors of the rainbow underneath the rotating lights above. She smiled and swayed to the music. "Ticket, please."

"Hello, Chesiree." I read her name tag and raised the phone. "The man upfront already scanned it."

"Yep, he scans you before you walk into the room. I scan you before you get on stage."

I had no plans to get on stage, but before I could tell her, she scanned the ticket on my phone.

She mouthed the words of the song as she looked over the tablet. She pushed a bright pink lollipop into her mouth, pushed it to one side, and said, "Ooh, Archangel Adam. Nice name. Haven't heard that one before." She scrolled down the tablet.

Hearing the name Adam caused my heart to beat faster. It was the nickname Eve had given me when we decided we'd start the world anew with our ideas.

Chesiree pulled the candy out of her mouth. "I'll be honest, honey. I don't think you're winning tonight. She's unstoppable! And between you and me," she leaned in and whispered, "I think the guys are rooting for her so that nobody gets her."

"Who is she?" I didn't mention that I knew little about what was going on because I didn't want to set off any alarms.

She recoiled and froze for a moment. "Are you kidding? You paid half a million dollars to compete against her."

That was news to me and further piqued my interest. Someone had gone to great lengths to set this up. My impatience for the result increased.

Chesiree shook her head and looked at me like I was insane. "You're up against the infamous Eve."

I grabbed the woman's shoulders. "Did you say Eve?"

She looked scared and ready to scream, but broke away instead when I looked up at the stage.

I couldn't see the singer's face. Her petite frame and long, black, and braided hair resembled the Eve I met two years ago. But that wasn't enough for me to believe that the woman on stage was her. I had to get closer and verify.

I ran to the steps that led up to the stage. I focused on the singer in case she turned around, so I didn't see the two bouncers until I collided with them.

"Eve? Eve!" The singer turned around in a long, mid-calf-length dress stained with grease or oils. She wore gray slip-on shoes, but her feet might as well have been bare based on their condition.

Chesiree pushed me forward from behind. "Go! Go!"

The bouncers let me go.

I stumbled forward, skipped a couple steps, and vaulted over the gate. The crowd, the music, and everything else stopped.

"Eve?" I knew the woman was Eve, but I wanted to hear her say it. She did without words when she dropped the microphone. When her eyes enlarged, her lips trembled, and her chest rose and fell at an irregular pace. Then I saw it—the metallic collar around her neck. Its silver lining blemished by what I believed were tears. My heart sank to a new low.

"Ladies and gentlemen, let me introduce you to the Archangel Adam!" Chesiree thrust the microphone to my chest. "If you can win the crowd, you can save her from this place." In a flirty, harmonic tone, she added, "Don't screw this up."

I held onto the microphone. The thought of freeing Eve from that place rang louder than the crowd and my pounding heart. I raised the microphone to my lips and walked toward Eve. The only song that came to mind—the only one I knew—was something my mother sang to me long ago. I remembered every word.

I believe that we can shine brighter than the stars in the sky

Eve didn't move. Her eyes followed me as I walked up to her, reached for and took her hand in mine. She didn't stop me from getting close, and she didn't step back, either.

And I believe that we can make a better world out of all this ice

Eve opened each finger of her fist and slipped them between mine. She placed her left hand on my shoulder and let me pass an arm around her.

Warm all the things that weigh us down
And shape the future with our eyes

We danced around the stage. Glided. Flew. Twirled like a flower that fell from a tree while all the leaves watched.

Just you and me against the world
We'll make a place for you and I

I removed my hand from her waist and brought our interlocked hands down as I lowered to one knee.

A place for you
A place for me
A place for...us

"Evelyn Grace, will you be my Valentine?"
Tears glistened on Eve's cheeks. She pulled at her dress as if she were trying to be more presentable. "It'll require more energy than before. I'm missing old parts and gained new ones."
I caught her free hand before she could touch the collar. "That makes two of us because I was lost without you." I rubbed my thumb across her knuckles.

Eve knelt on both knees and wrapped her arms around me. She pulled me into her embrace and said, "I'll fix us both."

⧗

Eve and I had walked off the stage hand in hand. Chesiree cheered us on the entire way, along with the crowd, before she called on the next competitors. A Karaoke worker led us to a counter where an older woman with thick glasses looked at us above the rim.

"Inmate 2493—"

"Evelyn Grace Valentine," I said, and dropped my hand on the counter to get the woman's attention. "Her name is Evelyn Grace Valentine."

Eve tightened her grip. She stared at our clasped hands until I pushed her black locks aside to reveal the collar. She flinched when I reached for it.

"I'd like this removed," I told the woman.

She slammed her stamp on a document. "It don't work like that, honey. That collar ensures she follows the rules. From this point forward, she's your responsibility. You'll serve—"

"I understand how the CARPE program works." I spoke with an angry voice. My name was clear as day on the paperwork, but the woman didn't recognize it to know that my dad pioneered the stupid program. "How do I remove it?"

The woman raised a brow when she looked up at me. She leaned back in her chair and folded her arms in defiance.

Eve grabbed my arm and pulled me away from the counter.

I whispered to her, "I'm sorry."

She rubbed my upper arm.

"I just wanted to get it off you. Somebody has the key. There's no way they'd make something you can never take off."

She smiled. "I can take it off. It's my design, reimagined by the lowest bidder."

I raised a brow. "So, you could've saved yourself?"

"I was planning to when the time was right. But this…this feels right."

D.5 Path of Uriel

The group was mostly quiet during Nathan's story. Michael and Kieran seemed to reflect on their history with Nathan. None of the other versions of Nathan had told them the story. Or maybe none of the other versions of Kieran had asked.

Uriel had shaken her head and smacked her lips multiple times. Siren stared at the ceiling with her feet in the air, their soles pointed toward the center of the platform. Aurora listened as if she were grading Nathan's decisions.

"I married the love of my life," Nathan said. He straightened his posture. "Well, not officially, but who determines that anyway?"

He looked at Michael and Kieran. Other versions of him had promised to help them find love if they helped him save Eve, which was ironic in my case, because Eve helped me find Siren.

I asked, "Why was Eve imprisoned?"

Nathan ran a hand through his hair on the left side of his head. "Someone had set her up. I was afraid if we talked about it, she'd break down, seek revenge, or something. So we left Eden and found a tiny house in the west—our happily ever after. It was like we'd retired and found peace at last. I thought we'd escaped everything."

"That's where she developed the temporal field?" I asked.

Nathan nodded. "Eve was all about her gadgets. She was always making something—"

Uriel jumped from her seat, dashed across the platform, and kicked Nathan in the chest. He fell to the ground, chair and all, and then scrambled to his feet. Uriel tossed the chair out of the way as she pursued him. "You fucking coward. You didn't trust she could handle the conversation."

Kieran and Michael stood ready to intervene. I shook my head at them, and they seemed to understand that differences needed to be resolved before we faced Evelyn, because she might've encountered a similar struggle and used it against us. So long as Uriel didn't kill Nathan.

Nathan stood toe to toe with Uriel. In a deep, grim tone, he said, "You really don't know what you're talking about. I took Eve away so that nobody could get to her."

Uriel put both hands on her hips and looked up at Nathan. "Sounds like you were afraid of Daddy. It's obvious that he put her in there. So you ran away instead of facing the problem like a—"

Nathan walked away. He headed for the garage door at a brisk pace.

"And there you go, running away again." Uriel folded her arms.

Nathan stopped, turned around, and stomped back toward her. "I don't have time for your tantrums, and I have no interest in being your definition of a man. The only opinion that matters is—"

"Eve's. Eve. Eve. Eve. That's the extent of your vocabulary. You're so obsessed with what she was that you never stopped to—"

Nathan bellowed, "I've loved her for over two hundred years."

Uriel lowered her voice to a frightening calm. "And in all that time, you never asked her if she was okay. Never talked about it. You know she's out there trying to create a version of you that would, right?"

Nathan's face softened, and his overbearing presence weakened.

Uriel added, "Of course you did. You know everything about Eve." She walked back across the platform and dropped into her chair, her eyes steady on Nathan.

I wheeled to the downed chair, leaned over, and flipped it upright.

Nathan sat with both elbows on his knees, and his face in his hands. Then he pushed his hair back and away from his face. His tears moistened the strands and temporarily kept them in place. "We just wanted to be together. Fuck." He rubbed his hands against his flight suit pants. "Eve probably knew my father was involved. She had a plan before I rescued," he air-quoted, "her, and I never asked what it was. We should've faced him sooner. Together. But losing would've meant putting that collar back on Eve. I just… I wasn't willing to take that risk."

I patted Nathan's shoulder because I couldn't reach over his broad physique to his back. "I understand your pain. To form this team, we had to decide which Kierans and Auroras to save, which meant leaving so many others to die." I looked at Siren and then down at my legs. "It wasn't a simple decision. But we made it because we didn't have any other choice." I wheeled back a few feet. "Just like our decision to bring you here, despite the risk of alerting Evelyn. With what you've told us about Eve and your temporal modulator, we can save her together."

"My what?" Nathan asked.

Michael walked up to Nathan and pointed at his own left arm.

Nathan understood and rolled back the sleeve to reveal the temporal modulator. The silver brace's light blue screen illuminated like a device exiting sleep mode.

Michael didn't seem happy to see the vambrace again. His gaze was distant for a moment. He said, "The Nathan I encountered said he fought back with the temporal modulator when TIME attacked him. Despite losing, the assailants didn't take it from him. Why wouldn't they take such a powerful device? Because they needed him—you—to use it and return to the future. Then the cycle starts over again." Michael sighed. "She knows you well."

Aurora abruptly stood. "Good luck," she said and walked to the door.

"You're leaving?" Kieran asked.

Aurora nodded. "Yeah. I'm not going to help the person responsible for my mother's death. The collar's creator and the world can end for all I fucking care." She walked out and slammed the door before we could respond.

Nathan stared at the door for a moment before he asked, "What did Eve do to her?"

I wheeled around to his front and waited for him to face me. "A VAC killed her mother. And across the various timelines, Auroras and Uriels wore the same VAC that Eve created."

Kieran jogged to the door.

"Leave her," Siren said.

Kieran grabbed the handle. "I can't just leave her," he said. He looked over his shoulder at Siren. "Weren't we just chastising Nathan for ignoring Eve?"

Siren passed her legs back over the chair's armrests. She placed the empty bottle of wine next to her and stared at the last drop in her glass. "I mean, don't ignore her for a hundred years. She'll be back."

"How do you know?" Kieran asked.

She cocked her head to the side, shifted her knees out of the way, and raised a brow at him. "She's me, remember? Sometimes we just need time to think about shit."

Nathan removed the modulator from his wrist and placed it in Michael's hands. "No more hesitation."

Michael inspected the modulator as he took it to the desk. "Now that I have an original, I'll modify it to work with the spatial modulator so we can control both simultaneously." He plugged it into a computer using a green USB mini cable. "The spatial modulator uses energy to collapse two points and tear a hole in space. Based on what you said about Eve's prototype, the temporal modulator uses similar energy to manipulate the speed of nearby objects and to move particles through the temporal barrier—across time."

Nathan had an expressionless face after he sat down. "You figured all that out from a story?"

Michael's eye reflected the monitors. "Not entirely. I've fought against the temporal modulator before when you tried to stop time." He glanced at Nathan and then pulled up the modulator's file system.

Nathan addressed me. "That was the plan then. So what's the plan now?" he asked.

I watched Nathan's body language, unsure whether we could trust him. The flat tone in his voice didn't help. I'd seen him betray Kieran many times, but this was different. An original model sat in front of me. Evelyn hadn't manipulated or set him off course.

With the temporal modulator in hand, I wondered if we needed his help in the upcoming battle. We did. I had forgotten the other reason we brought Nathan to this space-time. Kieran reminded me that there was one thing Nathan could do better than any of us.

Kieran walked away from the door. He stopped at the center of the platform and looked over his shoulder at Nathan. "We're hoping you can distract Evelyn long enough for us to remove her temporal and spatial modulators."

Uriel smirked. "Destroying them is my job. I kicked Nathan's ass before, so now it's on to the boss."

Nathan folded his arms. His muscles flexed. "You said you were trying to save Eve."

Uriel silenced me with a raised hand. "Yeah, but I ain't dying trying to do that. Keep her busy. I'll blink in and remove each modulator. Do your part and maybe nobody gets hurt."

Nathan stared at Uriel and then looked over her head at the monitors. "I know how to get her attention." He turned to, but looked through, me at the muted news broadcast on the monitor behind me. "I'll need to go home first."

I waited for Nathan's eyes to focus on me. "Evelyn could be here any minute. Bringing you to this space-time likely alerted her. We need to be ready."

Nathan walked over and stood by the exit. "I can't face Eve with words alone. To appease a goddess, you bring her an offering."

"What kind of offering?" Kieran asked. He walked off the platform on the side closest to Nathan.

Nathan folded his arms. "I'm going to destroy House Valentine."

Nathan and Kieran stared at each other for a few moments, each probably waiting for the other to back down. After neither did, Nathan said, "That should get national media attention. When the cameras are on me, I'll tell the world how to disable the collars."

None of the video I watched from other timelines suggested Nathan knew how to do that, but in his story, he'd mentioned Eve took the collar off herself. She must have told him how to do it.

Uriel huffed and puffed from her seat, so I asked before she could, "If you knew how to disable the collars, why didn't you?"

Nathan lowered his chin and turned toward me. "How would I have done that? Who would have believed me? By the time I convinced anybody about the VAC's vulnerability, DIEM would have patched it."

Michael raised his voice above the clattering of keys. "I can't disagree with him there."

Nathan took several steps away from the door. "I'm just now realizing that disabling the collars was likely a part of Eve's plan. She sang a specific song to disable hers—a vulnerability she hid inside the VAC's code before my father removed her from the project and imprisoned her."

"And nobody noticed?" I stroked my chin.

Nathan asked, "Do you always delve into another programmer's code if it already works?"

"Yes," all the Kierans said in unison.

Nathan shrugged. "When Eve taught me programming, I mostly copied and pasted what she had already written. Maybe I was a terrible student. But the engineers who completed the collars must have done the same; otherwise, she wouldn't have been able to disable her own." Nathan looked at his palm and then curled the fingers in. "We should have done something sooner, but after living in the temporal field, the rest of the world mattered less and less. Similar to living in the countryside with no signal. Over time, the plan went by the wayside."

Uriel lobbed her chair across the room and into the wall next to the door. I flinched, Kieran ducked, and Nathan swayed back as the chair broke. Two legs flew in separate directions. The rest of the chair crashed to the floor.

"By the fucking wayside?" Uriel shouted.

Kieran stopped her halfway across the platform. "I think he gets it."

"No. No, he fucking doesn't. Does he know how many people suffered and died because of that thing? Hundreds. Thousands. Hundreds of thousands!"

Nathan stepped away from the debris. "You know how to remove handcuffs, right? Have you ever kicked down the police station's doors to free the hundreds of thousands of innocents rotting in jail?" Nathan raised his voice. "And what do you think I'm trying to do now? People like you are the problem I was talking about. I mention disabling the collars and you attack me. If we were out there," he pointed toward the door, "DIEM would've patched the collars while you were throwing chairs at me and spouting nonsense."

Uriel stood down. She glared at the pillars, and I felt relieved when she didn't punch one. Siren walked over and escorted her to the far back corner of the room.

I addressed everyone. "We can't keep fighting each other. We're all upset, but now isn't the time. Evelyn is literally about to merge multiple dimensions and, well, you know." I waited for my words to settle. "We need each other."

Nathan shifted his narrowed eyes at me. "You asked me to help because I know Eve best. Actions speak much louder than words to Eve, and logic overrides emotion most of the time. She doesn't do something because she loves me; she does it because doing so will generate a chemical reaction that causes me to be happy."

I didn't want to argue with Nathan, because he knew Eve best, but I doubted how much he knew Evelyn. The time that had passed, and the merges she'd completed, had changed her. Once again, I found myself without enough time to make a sound decision. But there were more of us now. I didn't have to cycle through all the options alone. Kieran offered a solution.

"I'll go with you," he said.

Nathan shoved the debris aside with his foot. "I don't need a babysitter."

"No, you don't. But I know someone in Gabriel who can better execute your plan."

Nathan raised a brow like he was unconvinced. "Who?"

"Camille. She was an idol, Vocalist, and activist against the VAC in my timeline. Assuming she's similar here," Kieran looked at me and I nodded, "she'll know how to reach millions of households at the same time. Better than the media."

Nathan's face drooped. "I just told you how I plan to do that."

"So you're going to cause a disruption and then sing on the news?" Kieran shook his head in disbelief. "If VoCAl gets to the scene first, you won't stand a chance. And they will get there first."

"VoCAl doesn't have jurisdiction in the Heavens," Nathan said.

Kieran walked off the platform. "I've seen them make deals before. Either way, my method is less risky and will reach a wider audience faster." Kieran glanced at me. "I think doing this will also mean a lot to Aurora and Uriel."

"Whatever," Nathan grumbled.

I concurred. "Siren, Uriel, Michael, and I will get things ready here. Good luck."

⧗

One hour later, an alarm rang from the computer stations. Michael raised his hands and claimed innocence. I wheeled up to the desk and checked the error messages on the screen. Multiple windows, reminiscent of adware back in the day, popped up one after another. They all read: Signal lost. I turned to the monitors at the back wall. Several had gone blank. "No...no! Siren! It's starting. Evelyn is collapsing timelines!"

Siren leapt from her chair and bolted across the platform. "What the fuck? Why? Wasn't she supposed to come here?"

"Shit. No. I messed up. Evelyn looks for Nathan in a new timeline at the primary divergent point where she always placed him. She must've gone there, didn't see him, or a new timeline, and figured something was wrong." I panicked as more monitors went blank. Error messages flooded the screen until I instructed additional pop-ups to collapse into one. "We got her attention in the worst possible way."

"What do we do? What can I do?" Siren implored.

"Get the gateway ready!"

Uriel smacked her fist into her palm, ready for a fight. I wasn't sure she understood how powerful Evelyn was, but I said nothing. Her high spirits were required, and I hoped Michael's change to the modulators was going to raise Uriel to Evelyn's level.

"Michael, are the modulators ready?"

"Almost," Michael said. "I'm waiting on the power crystals, too. They are eighty percent charged."

"Start showing Uriel how to use them. She's our fighter. I'm going to delay Evelyn, and there's a very real possibility she'll come here immediately afterward."

"Delay Evelyn? How?" Michael asked.

I looked at him, but said nothing. He understood. His posture sagged as if his soul had departed. He looked over at Siren, who ran back and forth across the platform, plugging cables back into their connections.

Uriel figured it out, too. Her feisty attitude subsided.

"I'll need that chair you're sitting in and a little help to get into it," I said to Michael, and then wheeled down to the platform.

Siren twisted the last cable in place and stood ready. "What are we doing? What's next?"

I faced her. "Siren," I started, but stopped. I smiled at her energetic eyes and held back tears to avoid blurring the one thing that was crystal clear to me.

Siren cupped my face with both of her hands. "We're going to get through this."

"I need to go." I wanted to tell her everything at once, but choked after I started. I touched her hands and rubbed them.

Her eyes darted back and forth between me and Michael. "I don't understand," she said when she saw Michael position a chair at the center of the platform.

"Evelyn is ending the world and…" I inhaled and avoided eye contact. Siren grabbed my face with her hands and forced me to look at her. I exhaled. "I think I can slow her down."

Siren stepped back and smiled half-heartedly. "Okay, so what are we waiting for?" She placed a hand on her hip. "I don't understand, but you're scaring me, and it's pissing me off right now."

I steeled my resolve. "I'm going to the past—to where it all began—the primary point of divergence to be the voice in the back of my mind. If only for a few seconds, I'll convince myself to delay the first activation of the gate and disrupt time long enough to cause ripples. Since the merging of timelines requires precise timing, a few seconds should force her to recalculate."

Siren stared at me with a blank expression. "Okay. Do it. We'll pull you back after."

I shook my head. "Baby, there is no coming back." Siren's eyes widened, but I didn't stop—couldn't stop. "I have to merge with the original singular Kieran from the core timeline; before the very first activation of the gate." I frowned and then reiterated what ran through my head a hundred times to make sure I missed nothing. "A merge is required to avoid unraveling a new timeline, because a new timeline won't cause a ripple."

Siren glanced at the computer desks. "We have the temporal modulator. We'll just use it to get her attention."

"You know Evelyn doesn't respond to temporal distortions when Nathan isn't involved. To her, our actions are insignificant in the grand scheme, and we can't wait for her to decide that we're important. We have to act now."

"There has to be another way." She grabbed the armrests of my chair. "You're not doing this, Kieran." She firmly stated. Her grip on the armrests caused the veins across the back of her hands to be visible.

"I have to—"

"Why you? Why not…" she looked around, but didn't want to volunteer anyone else.

"It has to be me," I whispered.

"No, you're not doing this. I won't let you—"

Uriel passed her arms under Siren and lifted her up.

Siren kicked and screamed. If not for the pain in her heart that burst out in tears, she might've overcome Uriel's hold. But her body crumpled as she cried out.

"Please! Don't do this."

I closed my eyes. "I'm ready, Michael."

"No!"

I couldn't shut out Siren's screams. Every wail drew a picture of her in my mind. My heart broke with every cry. Tears streamed down my cheeks despite my best efforts to suppress them.

Michael lifted me from my chair and onto the one at the center of the platform. I squeezed my eyes shut, but knew I had to open them. To merge with myself, the position, posture, and breath had to be the same. Only *I* could come close to mimicking the original Kieran's demeanor—that moment he took a deep breath and stared at the computer's camera lens. That meant I had to lift my head and face Siren like she was five viewers that watched me.

Siren settled down. She either knew time was short, or she pretended to surrender. I could never tell, which was one more thing I loved about her. Siren was unpredictable, a welcomed difference from the predictable behavior of the systems I worked with daily.

I wanted to hold her hand, but I couldn't. I wanted to kiss her one more time, but didn't want her fresh scent, sweet taste, and rosy lips to disrupt the merge. They would be a wave against the shore. There was so much I wanted to tell her, but settled for brevity. "Siren, you're everything I ever wanted and more. I love you with every particle in my body."

Michael activated the system. It hummed and light flickered along the poles.

"Please don't. I need you," Siren whispered.

"You love me. And I love you." I smiled at her amber eyes. "Technically, our love transcended time."

"Fucking...nerd..." Siren forced a smile for me.

"Goodbye, Aurora Williams."

D.6 Path of Heavens

The back of my head throbbed, and the steady beep of an alarm didn't help. The last thing I remembered was riding column Gabriel's elevator with Nathan. He wanted to make an offering to Evelyn when she showed up by sabotaging his family name, or something like that, and then disabling Voice-Activated Collars around the city by singing a song. I had a better plan for disabling the VACs, so I followed him to get into column Gabriel and find Camille. Williams, Michael, Uriel, and Siren stayed behind to prepare for Evelyn's arrival.

But I couldn't recall walking out of the elevator and wondered why I opened my eyes to dim emergency lighting and one flashing strobe light behind me. After I adjusted my slouched posture to sit up straight, I saw Aurora and Camille on a couch across from me.

Aurora rested her chin in her palm, and her elbow on her knee. She was not amused. Every few seconds, her eyes followed one of the men and women tending to the wounds of the injured, working in the nearby electrical panel, standing guard, or restoring order. Yet no one had silenced the alarm.

Camille wore a pale green dress that draped over her crossed knees. She sat next to Aurora with both elbows resting on the top of the couch.

"Hey," Camille said. She bobbed her hanging foot. Initially, to get my attention, and in rhythm thereafter.

"What happened?" I asked.

I went to rub my head, but a man with blue latex gloves stopped me. He squatted in front of me, straightened my posture, and peered into each of my eyes.

He said, "We found you on the floor in the elevator. I would say you fell and hit your head on the way down, but it looks more like someone clobbered you first. Can you tell me your name?"

"Kieran." I looked at Aurora and repeated, "Kieran."

"Who is the current president?"

I stumbled on the question. Telling him I was from another timeline would have caused him to misdiagnose me. "Um, I don't know."

"Do you know the two ladies sitting across from you?"

I knew the light that flashed into my left eye. Very bright. Very annoying.

"Camille and Aurora." I blinked and then closed both eyes. The light was bright even with my eyes closed, so I waited for total darkness before I reopened them.

The lobby triggered reality. "Nathan! Where's..." The look in Camille and Aurora's eyes silenced me. "What happened?"

"We should get him to a hospital," the man said. "He's got a concussion."

"No, I'm fine." If I went to the hospital, I'd have missed the battle of a lifetime over a minor concussion.

Camille excused the paramedic. He left without question, moved to another man near the front desk, and asked similar questions.

Aurora watched the man walk away. When the surrounding chaos forgot about the three of us, she said, "Your boy Nathan knocked you out, took down the guards, sabotaged the power, which disabled the elevators, and then ran towards column Michael."

I shook my head and punched the side of the armrest with the broadside of my fist. I paused for a moment, and then asked Aurora, "Why are you here?"

"Same reason as you, I suppose. Camille was going to help me do what we did on Gabriel."

Without Nathan's temporal modulator, her voice wouldn't have had the same effect. I wondered if Aurora knew about the VAC's innate vulnerability. She hadn't been in the room when we discussed it. I noticed several collars on the security guards and a group of women barely wrapped in pool towels. Two rich snobs shouted commands at the paramedics.

"There's a better way." I leaned in and whispered, "You can disable them by singing a certain song." I sat up and placed both hands on my head. "Oh no, Nathan is the only one who knows the song. I have to get to him before the VoCAls do."

"Go for it," Aurora flatly said. "I know the song. Eve told me." Aurora shifted her eyes away and then back. "The good Eve," she added.

I turned my head too hard. It cracked and sent pain down the back of my neck. "Eve was here?" I asked after I moaned.

Aurora nodded.

"Where is she now?"

Aurora shrugged. "She said something was wrong and vanished."

I couldn't tell if Aurora stopped caring, or if she was no longer fazed by the manipulation of time and space.

Camille had remained silent. Her attention jumped between Aurora and me like a pinball in a machine. The look in her eyes suggested our conversation fascinated her.

"Does she…know?" I asked Aurora, but nodded at Camille.

"I do," Camille said with charm. "I almost didn't believe any of it, but the Eve you spoke of enlightened me. Otherwise, I wouldn't have let you up." Camille glanced around the room. "I'm still debating whether or not it was a good idea."

I apologized, and then said, "So Eve is aware of our actions. I wonder if she can see us the same way Williams sees the other timelines. If so, why doesn't she act or do more?"

Aurora further apologized to Camille on my behalf. "Don't take it personally. He gets like this sometimes. But when he sets his mind to something, he sees it through."

My body complained after I stood up. "I have to get to Nathan."

Camille summoned one of the attacked guards. "Grant, will you help Kieran get into column Michael?"

I remembered Grant from my previous timeline. He had objected to Nathan's crass manner of speech toward Camille.

Grant hesitated. "Ma'am, I'm not sure—" He paused. "Ms. Camille, I am not authorized to enter column Michael at this time. And I'm not sure we can trust this man." Grant sized me up.

Camille bounced her leg up and down. "Mr. Valentine's life is in danger." She steadied her leg and looked up at Grant. "Which is worse, answering to Gabriel or to Michael?"

Grant gritted his teeth and nodded his head toward the doors that led to Michael.

"Thank you, Camille. Aurora."

⌛

Grant and I ran across the roof of Gabriel. The run felt nostalgic. Several hours ago, I had raced with Aurora across the same green turf as VoCAIs chased us. In my previous timeline, the VoCAIs didn't have jurisdiction or immediate access to the Heavens. I hoped the same was true here, or that Camille could delay them long enough for me to find Nathan.

Halfway to the lobby connecting Gabriel's rooftop to Michael, the same flashing strobe light caught our attention. Grant pulled out a pistol and checked the chamber for a round.

"You're not going to shoot him, are you?"

"If I have to, I will. He's armed. Took a gun from one of my guys."

Grant slowed down twenty feet from the lobby entrance. He spoke into his wrist, "This is Gabriel security to Michael security. Can anybody hear me?" He motioned me to stand behind him and tip-toed over the broken glass at the entrance. "What the fuck happened here?"

Carnage. Bullet holes decorated the walls in every direction. Several men lay on the floor unconscious, possibly dead.

Grant checked their vitals one by one. "Thank God, nobody's dead."

I was eager to get going, but I didn't know which floor Nathan was on and didn't have the credentials to use the elevators, which were also disabled.

"Why, Nathan? How were you planning to escape if you broke all the elevators?" I asked myself aloud.

"Come on, there's a service elevator back here." Grant pointed to a corridor behind the lobby desk. "It's how security and housekeeping get around."

We walked around the desk and found the clerk cowering in fear behind it. She was a middle-aged woman with short white hair that was partially covered by the uniform jacket she hid under.

Grant knelt next to her. "Hey, I'm from Gabriel. It's okay. Help is on the way. Can you tell me which floor Mr. Valentine is on?"

She stopped shaking long enough to say, "Floor 665."

"Thank you. Keep your head down."

I followed Grant to the service elevator. He checked his gun two more times. After we reached the designated floor, he took a deep breath before the doors opened. The floor didn't look any different from the rooftop, and the ceiling was at least thirty feet high.

We saw the main elevators to our right. They faced an indoor courtyard leading to the house's entrance. The service elevator we used stood behind several trees that lined the edge of the room. Birds chirped from the branches above us after we stepped out onto more turf. Grant held his arm out and signaled for me to wait. I looked over his shoulder and saw Nathan standing in the middle of the courtyard.

Nathan's stance was stiff and serious. He held a pistol in his right hand, pointed at the ground. He was talking to someone. I couldn't see who, but their voice was loud and clear.

"I sacrificed everything to be here," a strong, older, masculine voice bellowed. It continued, "I sweated, bled, and killed for decades—centuries—to get here—to be here. I reformed the prison system, armed the police force with voice control, and earned my place in Michael. So why are you here, too?"

Nathan didn't respond, but his glare sent chills down my spine. I had never seen him like that before and hoped he would never turn those cold eyes on me.

The man chuckled. "You didn't know I would be here—that I was alive. You're just as blind as the day you married that wench and gave her my name! Yet, somehow, you've lived as long as I have."

A long silence followed.

"So what now? Are you here to claim an inheritance?" The man asked and then laughed. "Boy, I disowned you centuries ago. The entire world knows I threw you away."

At last, Nathan spoke. "I'm not here for inheritance, forgiveness, or apologies. I'm here to end you." Nathan raised the gun and fired it four times.

There was no time to react. The reverberations rang through my ears, further echoes absorbed by the sprawling vegetation.

"Nathan!" I ran out from behind the trees in time to see the man he was talking to collapse. I realized I had never seen Nathan's dad, only the image formed in my mind from Nathan's story.

Grant followed me into the open. He shouted, "Drop your weapon!" and aimed his pistol at Nathan, his finger shaky at the trigger. "Mr. Valentine? Sir, can you hear me?"

Nathan dropped his gun, not out of fear, but like he didn't need it anymore. He turned to me and seemed disappointed. "What are you doing here?"

Words froze on the tip of my tongue. I couldn't move. Nobody could move because Evelyn had arrived in front of the elevators that didn't work. She wore the same dark cloak as last time. It shrouded her body, but the hood was already down and her long black hair was out from under the scarf.

The conditions weren't right. Evelyn showed up when time was manipulated around, but not by Nathan. Nobody present could do that.

"Love?" Evelyn stalked Nathan, unsure that he was him. "No, he isn't supposed to be here. Not yet." She looked at me and seemed confused. "This is your doing, isn't it?" She paused. Her brown irises turned a gold hue. "You aren't supposed to be here, either."

I couldn't plead my case.

"This is my doing," Nathan said.

Evelyn smiled at him. She addressed him like he was a scared child, despite his confident voice and posture. "No, darling, it can't be. This is a mistake, something you're incapable of because you're perfect."

"Perfect?" Nathan smirked. "You got me." He raised both arms, amusement in his voice. "I'm always trying to catch up to what you are." He dropped both arms to their sides and frowned. "But clearly, I'm not there yet if you had to go through all this."

Evelyn's eyes darted back and forth across the space in front of her as she searched for a response. Her hands trembled. Her entire body seemed to fight between running and standing its ground. She was a far cry from the true neutral outlook she had once preached. Her behavior clarified that a Nathan aware of her path was a Nathan to be reckoned with.

A gunshot echoed throughout the room. Nathan stumbled forward and then down to one knee before he collapsed into Evelyn's arms. She had teleported to him.

Who had fired the shot? It hadn't been Evelyn. Maybe one of Valentine's guards had shown up and pulled the trigger. I could see the entrances, but everything beyond Valentine's body was outside my field of view because I couldn't turn my head.

I didn't need to turn my head. Valentine held a pistol in his left hand. He was on his feet. Alive! From his right hand, he dropped the four bullets Nathan had fired.

"Like I said, I disowned you *centuries* ago." He revealed two vambraces, very similar to the temporal modulator. "These babies gave me the time to build the empire I deserved by slowing my cell division." He lowered his arm and snarled at Evelyn. "And your presence, my dear, explains how he's survived all this time." He glanced at me and the birds frozen in mid-flight with a satisfied smile. "You enhanced the system to control a wider area. Very impressive. I will take that off your hands, after I kill you, too."

Evelyn focused on Nathan, but she heard the threat. "You should throw those away," she said.

Valentine laughed. "Why would I do that?"

"You are but a temporal slice of a whole. When I bring the slices back together, the variations in time among them will cause anomalies." Evelyn spoke in the same calm manner as when I had first encountered her. The frightened girl had gone with Nathan's bravado.

"You're not going to do anything but die and further my legacy!" Valentine fired two shots. They whizzed through Evelyn's temporal field and disappeared before they reached her. They reappeared through the side of Mr. Valentine's head and continued to vanish and reappear until they filed his skull down. The temporal field held his headless body frozen in place.

Evelyn caressed Nathan's cheeks. "Don't worry, love. This will all be over soon," she said, and vanished with him.

I completed my forward stumble and then vomited on the turf in front of me. My brain had processed all the imagery and sounds of Mr. Valentine's demise, but my body couldn't react. I wondered if that was the level of impact Eve wanted to have on the medical field.

Grant aimed his weapon wildly in front of him, and then at Mr. Valentine's headless body. He lost his cool. "What happened?"

I wiped my mouth with my forearm. "You wouldn't believe me if I told you." I walked over to Mr. Valentine, covered my nose, and looked away as

I pilfered both vambraces. His body fell to the ground after I jerked the last device away from his curled fingers.

Grant pointed his gun at me.

I raised both hands above my head, but didn't drop the vambrace. "You couldn't move, but you heard everything, right? Mr. Valentine aside, I have to stop Evelyn. We all die if I don't get to her. And I know you saw what she's capable of."

"What the... What the fuck is going on?" he shouted.

His twitchy trigger finger worried me, but he was only a flicker of flame to the conflagration of Evelyn.

"I don't have time to convince you, so if you're going to shoot me, do it. Otherwise, I need to chase her."

Grant took a couple of deep breaths and then lowered the gun.

I slid one temporal modulator on and cursed. "How am I supposed to find her, though? I should return to the garage, but I'd lose too much time. I can manipulate time, except only the surrounding time, not the entire world. I could go to the future, except there's no guarantee that the future me will be anywhere near the garage and I'd probably unravel the timeline and end up in another space-time. If only I had a spatial modulator." I walked in circles. On the eighth lap, I stopped and stared at the space Evelyn had occupied. "Wait, Evelyn doesn't unravel the timeline when she manipulates time. Grant, I need three extension cords, a power strip, and the current time."

Grant stood, dumbfounded.

"Now! Hurry!"

He ran into Mr. Valentine's home.

Neither modulator had the finishing touches of a commercial product. The exposed wiring and circuit boards seemed dangerous. None of them possessed a power crystal, which provided the energy required to traverse time. Instead, each had a 110 volt outlet integrated into the panel. That wasn't enough.

I stripped the shielding from the extension cords Grant brought and wired the leads into the modulator. "That should do it. I'm only going back ten minutes at most. What time did you get?" Evelyn's temporal field had stopped my watch. I subtracted its time from the readout inside the house, which was likely outside the field Evelyn had created. Then I calculated the exact time that I needed to go back to.

I placed my hand on the power strip's reset button and paused when Grant stood in front of me. "After I turn this thing on, I need you to go back and tell Camille everything you saw and heard. Give Aurora this." I updated the settings for the second modulator and gave it to him. "Tell her to put it on the microphone before she sings. It will modulate her voice and carry it farther."

"What are you going to do?" Grant asked, which gave me the idea that I should tell somebody what I was planning.

"You saw Evelyn—the dark-haired woman—disappear, right?"

Grant nodded.

"She teleported somewhere. I'm going back in time to the point when she disappeared, so she can teleport me, too." Then aloud to myself, "Which means I'll need to move forward in time after. To the present. I'll add a waypoint. I don't know if this'll work, but I have to try. Can you tell them all that, too?"

Grant nodded with confused eyes. I wasn't sure if he fully understood and I didn't have time to verify.

"Thanks, man. Sorry about all this." I stood where Evelyn had moments ago, entered the designated time, and flipped the power. "Here we go. Three… Two… One…"

D.7 Path of Evelyn Grace Valentine

Shit. I knew Evelyn's signature move was to suspend time wherever she went. Following her, I teleported into suspended animation. Behind the group. In the garage. The temporal modulator didn't have time to activate and send me minutes to the desired future.

The field immobilized the others, too. Their paused actions resembled mannequins in a clothing store. Everyone watched Evelyn carry Nathan to the center of the platform. She had suspended his movements, too. She adjusted his posture like the main attraction at the front of the store—body upright, arms to the sides, and head tilted down toward her. With artistic prose, she pushed the top of his eye sockets up, pulled his lip down slightly, and molded a suspenseful expression on his face using her fingers.

The platform's center was exactly where she had imprisoned him in the core timeline, which meant she was planning to collapse our timeline. And all we could do was watch. Despite our preparation, we hadn't overcome her most basic ability.

Time moved again. Evelyn had looked at the ceiling just before the modulator threw me minutes into the future.

"Nice of you to join us," Michael said from the desk behind me. He sat on the side close to the ramp. Minutes ago, he was strapping the modulators to Uriel's arms.

"Better late than never," Uriel said. She had a modulator on each arm and stood on high alert. She faced the empty platform Evelyn had suspended Nathan above earlier. "We need Siren. Aurora's voice won't last forever."

So, I asked you to keep it
This voice that was mistreated

I heard the song, which meant Grant had fulfilled his duty. Aurora used the temporal modulator to broadcast her voice across Eden, which probably intervened with Evelyn's temporal field and freed us from stasis. Grant had wasted no time.

I was in her voice's direct path this time, enchanted with hope, strength, and even love. Any aggression or anxiety I had vanished. The song seemed to lift the spirits of the others, too. They were full of energy despite the dire situation.

Uriel turned to her left and then back to the right, ready to swing at anything that showed its face. "Fuck! Where is she?"

"I'm working on it," Michael shouted above the rapid tapping of keys.

In hopes that you could heal it
Over time and you will find

"What's going on?"

"The bitch is fighting dirty," Uriel growled. "We need Siren!"

Michael translated, "Evelyn is dropping in and out of this timeline."

I scanned the room for Siren and found her sitting on the steps leading up to the kitchen, elbows on knees, and face buried between them. As I ran to her, I asked, "Where's Williams?"

Michael stopped typing. There was a long pause before he said, "He's watching over us in another space-time."

I saw his melancholic smile before I passed the desk and reached the stairs. "Siren!" I ran up the stairs and sat next to her. "Hey, what's wrong?"

"You left…" she said, her voice muffled.

"What?"

Siren raised her head hard and fast. She looked at me with angry eyes and drenched cheeks. "You left. The number one rule for a party is don't split up." She lowered her tone. "He taught me that." Then she burned a hole through my soul with her gaze. "Now he's gone. He made the ultimate sacrifice because *you* left."

I never thought that I could say
A single word that made your day

Tears welled in my eyes. Guilt played tug-of-war with the positive energy induced by Aurora's song. And when I couldn't decide how to feel, I felt my mind disconnect from my body. I couldn't feel anything physical. The pain was worse than Evelyn's stasis because parts of my mind ceased to function, too.

Michael shouted from below. "Siren, that's not true!"

Or anything that'd make you stay
By my side, all the time

"He was my reason for fighting," she said, and buried her head between her knees.

"Siren... I didn't... I mean..." Nothing I could say would bring Williams back. No excuse would console her. "I'm so sorry." I wrapped my arms around Siren. I wanted to cry with her, but our world could end any minute, and the others were counting on me.

Uriel shouted, "What if I go to the core and start pulling Nathans from there? I swear, I'll only pull the bad ones. 'Cause, fuck those versions."

My voice was something that you longed for
A treasure that you sought to explore

"I got it!" Michael snapped his fingers in Uriel's direction. "Downloading an update to your modulators now. Your temporal and spatial modulators will cycle frequencies of nearby timelines and respond to energy signatures matching Evelyn's activations. That will automatically dial your modulators to that space-time." Michael glided down the line of tables. "I also programmed your home coordinates to this timeline."

Uriel grinned. "We're definitely the best pair. I'm going after her!"

Words I never heard before
All my life before this time

"Update complete. Please come—"

"Shut up! Don't get sentimental on me." Uriel vanished.

"Back safely," Michael finished. He turned to me and tossed the goggles Williams had showed us earlier.

I caught them above Siren's head.

Michael rolled back to the other end of the table. "Eve showed up and took Nathan to another timeline just before you arrived. He looked hurt. Evelyn used her temporal modulator to slow his degeneration, which helped us fight back. That and Aurora's singing."

You said that it resonated
With all the things that you hated

"How is Evelyn still manipulating time?" I passed the goggle's straps around my head and rested the circular frames against my forehead.

"She learned to activate in-between Aurora's vocal vibrations. Those higher brain functions we talked about probably helped. On the bright side, Aurora slowed her enough to give Uriel a fighting chance and allowed Eve to swoop in and take Nathan."

Still, you refused to even trade it
For anything, or anyone

I lowered the goggles over my eyes. "What am I looking for?"

"Find Eve. She's trying to save Nathan's life. We'll still need him to distract Evelyn."

I cycled through the goggle's menu options while I spoke. "Aurora's voice is disrupting the goggles, too." Sort of. Enough of the signal got through and the resultant view was like a CRT TV experiencing interference.

I rested my index finger on a button next to the STOP indicator at the top right of my view. The goggles cycled through the dimensions on their own, like a radio set to scan mode.

I stopped in a timeline where Camille and I danced. That version of me had converted the garage into a ballroom. Hip-Hop music played in the background. I wondered if they knew what was happening around them, or if they knew our timeline could collapse on theirs at any moment.

I spent five seconds in each subsequent dimension. There were timelines where I sat alone in the garage, others where the garage was empty, but even more where Aurora and I enjoyed some activity together.

Was Aurora my soulmate, too?

I smashed the button to stop the scan. I almost passed the timeline Eve had retreated to with Nathan. She sat on the platform with his head in her lap and caressed his cheeks. Even though I could see her, I couldn't talk to her. How was I supposed to tell her anything?

Eve looked up at me, which made me wonder if the goggles worked both ways. The science didn't support that. The goggles were passive. Particles from other dimensions collected on the diamond, not transmitted. Eve could find us before. Maybe she had the same technology, but I didn't see goggles over her face.

Eve snapped her finger. I panicked after my vision went black. I scurried down the remaining steps of the stairs and then pulled the goggles up over my head. Eve stared at me like she wondered why I acted like a fool.

"Can you…hear me?" I asked.

She nodded. Her aura was pleasant and non-threatening. I had difficulty believing that any part of her could be or could become Evelyn.

"Am I…here? In your timeline?"

She pushed a few strands of black hair away from her pale face. "I transported you."

"You saw me? How did you see me?"

Eve tapped her sky-blue painted nail near the corner of her right eye. "Optical implants that function similar to your goggles."

Her eyes glowed the same way Evelyn's did; a rich gold hue, which scared me until they looked away.

"Is he…okay?" I sat on the step leading to the lower floor the platform sat on.

"I removed the bullet, but his fever's being stubborn." Her eyes glowed brightly again and then dimmed.

"What are you doing?"

"Accelerating cellular division. Helping his cells do their job. But cells will only divide so many times. I have to be careful that saving him doesn't shorten his lifespan."

Evelyn had merged with several of her variants. Our group discussed the psychological stress, but what were the physical impacts? If I merged with

Williams, would I be paralyzed, too? I asked, "What'll happen if he's merged with a shortened lifespan?"

"His impact alone will be insignificant. Changes to the whole will scale based on the number of parts suffering the same. This Nathan is a temporal fragment. The whole may lose a day, or an hour of his life." Eve frowned. "Which is an eternity for people like us, who love with everything we have every second of every day."

The room was as barren as the empty ones I'd seen. I wondered what had happened to the resident Kieran. Maybe he was on Gabriel, or Michael. Williams had said we frequented the same places.

I sat cross-legged and asked, "How do we prevent the multi-version of you from shortening our lifespans?"

"You've already figured that out. *He* is my weakness." Eve kissed Nathan's forehead. "But that window may have passed. You should've stopped her when she focused on his injury."

"Unfortunately, I wasn't there." I lowered my eyes and thought about Williams, and how I didn't even have time to say goodbye. "We could've used your help a few times."

"You're overestimating my strength. To help, I have to figure out what you're doing without alerting Evelyn. With so many unknown variables, it's difficult to calculate which of you stands a better chance at stopping her." Eve stroked Nathan's hair. "And if she finds and merges with me, she'll be unstoppable."

Eve had to make the same tough choices as Williams and Siren. Neither of us was qualified to make those decisions.

She looked at the wall where Williams had set up the monitors in his time. "I'm not strong enough to fight her. She has merged many more times than I have, most willing and some unwilling."

"And she collapses a timeline every time she merges," I added.

Eve shook her head. "Evelyn and I both can complete a merge without collapsing the timeline."

I sat up straight, ears perked, and head tilted in confusion. "Then why did Williams say she was trying to collapse the timelines?"

"A part of her hates the world for taking so much away from her. A part of her wants to save Nathan. Another wants to escape reality. Her actions are the combined efforts of the merged variants and their desires." Before I could digest what she said, Eve turned to me. "You can't stay here."

I had so many more questions. Nathan's story about Eve didn't prepare me for talking to her in person. Her energy was different. Pleasant. I could have talked to her for ages.

Eve canvassed the room like she was looking at another timeline. "She can track the signatures of temporal distortions the same way Uriel can. I delayed propagation of the energy signature that resulted from transporting you here, but I need to focus on healing him. I'll send you back and then move to another timeline."

"We need Nathan!" I shouted before Eve finished raising her hand.

"His life is no longer in danger, so her attention will no longer be divided. If I send him with you now, everything will end. Find another way." Eve looked at me with nostalgic relief. "I'm glad I chose you, Kieran."

Before I could ask more questions, or relish the emotions stirred by the way Eve spoke my name, she returned me to Williams' garage.

Eve transported me below Uriel and Evelyn as they exchanged blows above my head. Despite the quick exchange of punches, Evelyn had time to glare at me as if nothing escaped her field of view. She reached for me, but Uriel caught her arm and shoved her away. I scurried from the fight and slipped under the computer station desk to catch my breath. Uriel and Evelyn continued their fight, porting around the room and occasionally, in and out of the timeline. I saw them appear on one or two of the monitors, which meant Eve could show up on them, too.

Maybe she can't see other timelines the way Eve can.

Michael must have thought the same thing. He raced to the array of monitors and began unplugging them one by one. I shoved the goggles into my cargo pants to keep them out of Evelyn's hands.

After Michael disconnected several monitors, Evelyn teleported next to him and kneed him in the stomach from the side. Uriel caught up less than a second later and slugged her.

Both blinked to the center of the room, between the platform and the computer desks. Then the singing stopped.

"Fuck," Uriel said. She held her ribs and fell to one knee. After several deep breaths, she sang.

I believe, we can shine, brighter than the stars—

Evelyn snatched Uriel by the hair and kneed her in the throat.

Uriel choked, coughed up blood, and let out a harsh, wheezing after she fell to the ground. She shuffled her feet to get away and collided with the wall opposite the garage door.

Evelyn grabbed Uriel by the throat with both hands and lifted her up against the wall. "I didn't want to do that. Your voice is so beautiful, yet so detrimental to my path."

Uriel's feet dangled. She grabbed and punched Evelyn's arms, but couldn't break free.

"No!" Michael shouted. He tripped over the cables at his feet. One hand prevented him from falling over and the other nursed his stomach. "We surrender! We won't fight you anymore."

Evelyn didn't look at him. She focused on Uriel. "You've said that before, but you always interfere. You've also sacrificed yourself many times for her. Perhaps, this time, the sacrifice should be hers."

I joined the intervention, crawled out from under the desk, and raised the goggles into the air. "You want these, right? I'll smash them if you don't let her go!"

Evelyn looked at me. "No, you won't." She suspended everything for a moment before time resumed again.

Why? No Vocalist was singing.

Evelyn stared at one monitor from the array on the desk. A muted news broadcast showed celebrations across Eden. People held VACs in the air, smashed them on the ground, and hurled them into giant bonfires. VoCAls attempted and failed to quell the uprising. Aurora had succeeded.

A single tear ran down Evelyn's cheek. She closed her eyes tight as if to cut the flow. "No, it's another distraction. Don't let them distract us. We'll fix those later. Those things won't exist in my world!"

I passed the goggles over my head and around my neck. "So you created a problem, and now you're going to create your own world and abandon the people you impacted?"

"I didn't create…*that*." Evelyn tightened her grip around Uriel's neck, which forced an unhealthy shriek. "You did. They did. The people who have taken everything from me." She paused and an uncomfortable smirk formed. "I *should* take everything from them."

Uriel's face turned blue. But she hadn't given up. While Evelyn spoke, she patted down Evelyn's arms in every attempt to find and remove the modulators. She slid the sleeves up, shoved her fingers under the garment, and found nothing.

Evelyn didn't stop her. Instead, she grabbed the temporal modulator around Uriel's arm. "I'll be taking this back." She yanked the modulator free and broke Uriel's wrist. A loud pop synchronized with Uriel's discordant wail. Evelyn dropped her.

Uriel scurried around Evelyn's feet, using her good hand to maintain balance until she fell to the ground behind Evelyn. With a large, bruised grin on her face, she mouthed, "Boom." The temporal modulator exploded in Evelyn's hands after she turned around. The blast knocked Evelyn into the wall behind her.

Uriel struggled to her feet, coughing and spitting blood. "Fuck. It wouldn't be that easy," she grumbled.

The smoke cleared, but it was obvious before then that Evelyn was still standing. She took large, haggard breaths at first and then slowed them to an unsteady wheezing. The blast had torn half her clothes off. The upper left side of her body down to her forearm was naked. There was no modulator in sight. Nothing but the pieces of Uriel's modulator had clattered to the floor.

"She never had a modulator?" I crawled out from under the desks for a better look at Evelyn's left side. "They're implanted into her fucking skin?"

Small nodes ran up Evelyn's left arm, around her shoulder, and down her breast. Silver lines connected several nodes together and a few more ended at the base of her neck where the scarf had hidden them. The modifications explained her impressive reaction speeds and masterful control of time and space modulation.

I kicked myself for not having realized sooner, even after Eve told me about her own optical implants.

Michael ran along the garage door to my side of the room. "She's a genius with a lot of time on her hands. Another version of her could've done it before they merged. Who knows? But we underestimated her," he growled in a low voice.

She could've conducted the operation on herself if she used a temporal modulator the way she had envisioned—as a medical device. She could've slowed the signals to the pain receptors or sped up her healing after the operation.

I glared at her. When she noticed, she flashed her irises gold.

She took another deep breath and looked down at her charred skin. The left side of her face blistered, and red surrounded her now dimmed irises. The pain was clear in her eyes. She was hurt, but not defeated. Her eyes glowed again and steadied. Slowly, the smoke that rose from the burned skin dissipated, and the black and blue patches started clearing. The bleeding stopped. The wheezing dropped to healthier breaths.

"She's regenerating?" I moved closer to peer through the smoke that lingered. "She's accelerating cell division and healing."

Uriel spit more blood onto the concrete. She still had the spatial modulator and used it to teleport next to Evelyn. She drove a right hook into Evelyn's face. Then she scratched the nodes across Evelyn's body with her nails. Uriel tried to reveal and scrape Evelyn's right side, too, but her broken wrist made that impossible.

Evelyn grabbed Uriel's wrist and twisted it again. Uriel landed two more punches, but the rest never reached their mark. Uriel's auburn hair grew and turned gray at the roots. Her muscles tensed, but the strength in them drained. She hunched forward and grabbed hold of Evelyn for support.

Evelyn's gold eyes watched Uriel crumple to the floor. They never wavered, even after Michael begged her to stop. She aged Uriel and then shoved her into Michael after he dashed across the room to her aid.

"No, no… Aurora…," Michael cried. He stumbled backward and lowered them both to the ground.

Michael held Uriel in his arms. He caressed her wrinkled cheeks and pushed aside the gray strands, some of which fell to the ground. When his tears dripped on her, he desperately wiped them away. "It should've been me. I should've been fighting."

"You… You did…part…" she mumbled. Uriel took a deep breath. "At least I fought protecting someone I love." She touched his lips. "Someone I…loved…the rest of my…"

"Aurora. Aurora!"

Tears blurred my vision, too. I wiped them away to maintain a clear view of Evelyn. I knew Evelyn needed less than a second to act, but I couldn't ignore Uriel.

"God. FUCK!" Michael cried out. "Please. Come back." He rocked Uriel in his arms. Then he stopped. "Wait, Aurora, don't go. I can rewind time. I'll learn to rewind time."

"I already tried," Evelyn said. Her irises glowed again when she started healing. "I wanted to undo everything they did to me, but it was impossible. There's not enough energy or processing power to—"

"Go to hell!" Michael said.

Evelyn choked. "I have to complete the merge and then you will have the best parts of her."

"She was perfect the way she was. Not that you'd understand. You hate everything about yourself and Nathan. You're a fucking monster!"

I watched the pain in Evelyn's eyes amplify. The irises wavered, flickered on and off until she shook her head of the guilt that also caused her hands to tremble. "I will fix…everything… I promise—"

Siren tackled Evelyn. Before I could remind her about the aging Uriel just suffered, she unleashed a loud melodic wail that devolved into a deafening and painful cry. It felt like she focused all of her hate, rage, and pain at Evelyn without stopping to breathe.

I covered my ears and thought that closing my eyes would further muffle the scream. But I couldn't turn away from Evelyn. Not after the nodes in her skin sparked and tore from her flesh like fuse wire.

Both irises shorted, the pure gold hue faded to hazel and then to darkness. Even after Evelyn ceased moving, Siren didn't stop until her voice gave out. She didn't stop until she bellowed air and her scream turned into a haggard wheezing. Only then did she stop. She collapsed atop Evelyn and sobbed.

I ran to Siren because I wasn't sure Evelyn was down for good. I pulled her away from Evelyn, slipped under her right arm and helped her to the lounge she normally sat in. When I looked back at Evelyn, Nathan knelt next to her and Eve stood over her. Siren pushed me aside so she could see.

"Hey, beautiful," Nathan said. He touched Evelyn's colorless cheeks. He had a different aura about him. His existence was more prominent and his voice more harmonic.

Evelyn didn't respond. Maybe she couldn't respond.

Nathan took her trembling hand into his. "I'm so sorry. There are…so…so many things I should have done better. Things that we should have done…together."

Evelyn mouthed inaudible words before her breathing slowed and stopped altogether. Nathan kissed her scorched lips and closed her eyes. "I love you, too," he said.

Eve placed a hand on his shoulder. "*We* love you." She closed her eyes and lay down next to Evelyn. A few moments of silence passed before Evelyn's body disappeared.

Eve had merged with Evelyn. The damage from the recent battle was clear on Eve's body, the parts I could see. I remembered her explanation of the physical impact of merging. If only one version of Evelyn was battered, the bruises might not have appeared on

Eve. Since Evelyn comprised of many temporal versions, the scars on Eve were visible and so was the damage to her eyes.

"Eve?" Nathan said, his brows furled together.

Eve opened her eyes. She sat up and traced the fresh scars on her neck, winced from the pain of bruised cheeks, and hesitated to move her hands to her face.

Nathan caught her wandering hand before she could touch her eyes.

"It's my pain to bear," she said and looked in Nathan's general direction.

"Not alone. This time, we'll bear it together."

Eve leaned her head against Nathan's chest and smiled. "Are we starting over again?" She fumbled her hands around Nathan's upper body until he guided them to his face. "Hello, Nathan. My name is Evelyn Grace Valentine."

Path of Time

"I'm ready," I said. "Temporal Iteration: Michael. Project Title: Path of Time. Current time: 0055 hours. The initial run for record will begin at 0100 hours. The first objective…" I paused. For a second, I thought I saw Uriel from the corner of my eye, posted by the garage door, arms around her knees, watching me. Instead, Uriel was watching over me, and her temporal counterpart, Aurora, raised a brow at me. "Michael, was that thing on the entire time?"

With the weight of a world lifted from her shoulders, I'd finally met the real her, which wasn't a far cry from her sisters—the word we used to signify that we're family now. None of them minced words, applied filters, or held back. They spoke their minds, and Kieran and I wouldn't have it any other way.

I waved at the camera. "Dunno. If it was on, I'm pretty sure Evelyn's time manipulation cut the stream off long ago."

"So, it's good before then?" She sat cross-legged in the chair next to me and spun herself in circles. "We should keep it. It's the only actual memory we have of them."

There was an entire house above us, but we liked the garage. A chill air seeped in underneath the garage door when winter's herald blew in the evenings. There were fewer warm bodies, but that didn't make the room less cozy in the presence of family.

"What do you think, Siren?"

Siren sat in her usual lounge and stared at the blank monitors, wine glass in one hand and a small white board in the other. She wrote: You know I'll never forget them.

Aurora faced her. "Didn't the doctor say you should drink medicine instead of wine?"

Siren frantically scrubbed the board clean and scribbled: Blah, blah, blah.

We laughed. The others would've wanted us to. I know that because one of them was a temporal slice of me. Perhaps the best slice.

"On the bright side, yelling at us will require more effort," I said.

Siren didn't respond in writing. She simply raised a middle finger.

Aurora pushed off the desk enough to rotate a quarter turn. "What do you think about keeping the video, Kieran? Should we make a montage or something?"

Kieran paused his soldering. We had extended the original desk setup to give us more work space. He had accepted the side closest to the garage door, since neither of us wanted to remove the ramp on the other end. He raised his head and looked at us through the safety glasses.

"Even if the stream cut off, there should be a local copy of the video. I'd probably cry if I watched it," he said. He lowered the glasses and continued soldering. "That video is hours long. And not once did I tell them how much I love them."

Siren raised the white board above her head: I love you, Kieran.

Kieran's head was down, buried in his work, and Siren never turned around to see if he saw what she wrote. Neither of us needed to see the words. We said and wrote them still, so we'd never again regret keeping them inside.

Siren got up and walked over to Kieran. She wrapped her arms around him from behind and kissed the top of his head. She kissed Aurora on the forehead and did the same to me before she disappeared up the stairs.

Aurora completed a three-quarter turn back to me. "Do you think Nathan and Eve went back to the core timeline?"

I shrugged. I cared, and I didn't. The last few months had been about nothing but Nathan and Eve. Now that we had celebrated Williams's and Uriel's lives, I was ready to consider what should come next.

I asked Aurora, "Where do you want to go? What do you want to do?"

Aurora placed an index finger to her chin and spun the chair again, but slowly. "I want to protect our family. Disable collars across other timelines. Overthrow the VoCAIs." She stopped the chair when she faced Kieran. Then turned her head back to me. "I want to protect the timelines."

I grabbed the web camera and pointed it at Aurora. "Tell the world." I impersonated a young adult. "Thanks for saving us. Who are you guys?"

Aurora faced the camera, ruffled her amber curls, grabbed the chair in front of her crossed legs, and grinned. "My name is Aurora, and I am the majestic voice of the Temporal Interdimensional Multidimensional Enforcers."

Photo by Ervin Emmanuel

About the Author

KENNY EMMANUEL creates original science fiction and fantasy worlds that immerse readers in unique characters and settings, via short stories, novels, and video games. Visit www.kennyemmanuel.com to dive into more worlds.